BFF'S 3:

Best Frenemies Forever Series

BFF'S 3:

Best Frenemies Forever Series

Brenda Hampton

www.urbanbooks.net

Urban Books, LLC
97 N18th Street
Wyandanch, NY 11798

BFF'S 3: Best Frenemies Forever Series

ISBN 13: 978-1-62286-962-6
ISBN 10: 1-62286-962-1

First Trade Paperback Printing March 2016
Printed in the United States of America

10 9 8 7 6 5 4 3 2 1

Distributed by Kensington Publishing Corp.
Submit Orders to:
Customer Service
400 Hahn Road
Westminster, MD 21157-4627
Phone: 1-800-733-3000
Fax: 1-800-659-2436

BFF'S 3:

Best Frenemies Forever Series

Brenda Hampton

1

Evelyn

After being beaten up and almost killed by my lover, I was finally home from the hospital. It felt good to be in my own bed, without anyone poking me with needles or trying to tell me what I needed to do to get well. I was already feeling better, especially after my ongoing visits from my BFF's, Kayla and Trina. I was delighted and super excited that we were able to put our issues behind us and become friends again.

Our friendship journey had been a long one. We had had ups and downs, even a few betrayals. It shocked the hell out of me that Kayla had finally forgiven me for having sex with Cedric, her husband at the time, and, in addition to that, getting knocked up by him. I'd had an abortion, and at the time, I had felt as if it was something I needed to do.

Then there was Trina. Lord knows, I had done some reckless things to her too. I had interfered with her loving but shaky relationship with Keith, only because he had seemed as if he was trying to get into my panties. After further evaluation, I had realized that I was dead wrong. He appeared to love Trina to death. I had misjudged him, just like I had misjudged his brother, Bryson. Looks were deceiving, and he was the reason I had been in the hospital. When I said he had beaten my ass, I meant it. He. Had. Beaten. My. Ass. I had thought I was going to die that day. I had started seeing bright white lights, but thankfully, God hadn't been ready for me yet. Now that the dust had settled, and I was feeling 100 percent again, he was going to pay for putting his hands on me.

Bryson was upset because I had told a few people that I had caught him getting his freak on with a transgender man. Many people thought I was lying, but I would never spread a vicious rumor like that unless I had all the facts. I knew good and well what I had witnessed that day. He knew it too, but he continued to lie and make me look like the villain.

My intentions were to sue the hell out of him. His rich parents had already hired an attorney, and they truly believed that I was some kind of broke bitch who wouldn't be able to defend myself. While I didn't have much money—well, honestly, I was broke and didn't have a job—I still knew of one person in particular who had cash and was willing to help me out of this mess. He had come to rescue me while I was laid up in the hospital, feeling sorry for myself and worried about my situation. While Cedric and I unquestionably had our differences, those differences had been kicked to the curb and set aside for another day. According to him, he wanted to help me. And if he was able to, then I had no problem helping him.

I lay comfortably in my bed, with a fluffy pillow tucked between my legs, thinking about his brief visit at the hospital that day. Who would have thought that he would be the one to ultimately save me from what I was about to face with Bryson and his family?

Cedric strutted into the room with a card in his hand and a smile across his face. "Hey there, stranger," he said, walking farther into the room. "Baby, how are you feeling?"

Baby, my ass. Save it, *I thought. "Better," was all I said, trying to keep our conversation short.*

Cedric laid the card on the table, then sat in the chair beside my bed. He crossed his legs and massaged his hands. "So, when are you getting out of this place?" he asked.

My tone was very nasty. "In a few days. Why?"

"Because I kind of miss my partner in crime. Kind of need you to handle some things for me. If you do, there will be some great rewards."

I was slumped down in the bed, then sat up to give him my full attention. "What kind of things do you want me to handle? And I'd like to hear more about those rewards."

Cedric passed me an envelope and asked me to open it and read the letter inside. I did. It was a letter from Paula Daniels, the woman I thought had attempted to kill him. According to the letter, she wanted to speak to Cedric ASAP about his son, Jacoby's, involvement. That was all she said on the subject, but she also assured him that everything wasn't what it seemed to be. I slowly folded the letter and gave it back to Cedric. I wasn't sure what was going on, but I asked Cedric why he couldn't handle this.

"Jacoby is fragile, and Kayla is weak. I don't want to hurt anybody's feelings. Plus, I'm always being lied to. That's why I need you. I need someone like you to check things out for me, and since Kayla is back on your team, maybe you can find out what's really going on for me."

A part of me didn't want to be used by Cedric again, but I still wanted to hear about those rewards.

"If I do get involved, what's in this for me?"

"Depends."

"Depends on what?"

"Depends on what you want or what you need. Like a lawyer to help you fight your case, a new house, sex, whatever you want."

"Hmm, but you haven't said the magic word yet. The one thing that energizes me and turns me into the woman I always wanted to be. A rich woman."

Cedric snapped his fingers and smiled. "Oh yeah, that's right. I almost forgot. How could I forget about that? Money, right? However much your heart desires, as long as it's within reason."

I laughed, then shot him a slow wink. "It's a good thing that you know me so well, Cedric. But let me think about this. When I get out of here, I'll definitely be in touch."

The fortunate thing was, I hadn't waited until I got out of the hospital to put a plan in motion. I had spoken to Cedric almost every day since his visit. He had already made contact with Bryson's parents, and a meeting to try to resolve all this crap was scheduled for this Friday. I couldn't wait to tell his parents my side of the story—they definitely needed to hear what kind of animal their son was, if they didn't already know. I figured that Keith would be there too. That way, he would finally know the truth about his brother and stop hating on me.

He and Trina stayed into it about who was telling the truth. Keith took his brother's side; Trina took mine. But no matter whose side anybody was on, for the time being, I was glad about Cedric having my back. I made him aware that I didn't want Trina or Kayla to know that he and I had reconciled some of our differences. If they knew we were friends again, I was positive that they would think I was trying to betray them again and that they would cut me off. Then I wouldn't be able to get

Cedric the information he had requested about Jacoby and Kayla.

There seemed to be a big secret they had been keeping from Cedric. It revolved around him being shot. Paula Daniels was behind bars for the remainder of her life, but Cedric wasn't exactly sure that she was the one responsible for trying to take him down. If anybody knew the real deal, Kayla did. And if she had been keeping a secret, I was positive that I could get it out of her. Whatever information I found out, I intended to pass on to Cedric. It would be up to him to decide what to do with that information. After that, I wanted nothing else to do with him and our business would be done.

Friday was here before I knew it. I was well rested, and for the first time in a long time, I felt good about my future. I was currently unemployed, I didn't have much money in my bank account, and this apartment was starting to close in on me. I hated it here, but today I felt that a life-changing event was about to take place. Something inside told me that this meeting would work out in my favor.

Cedric was supposed to pick me up within the hour. I had been thinking too much about the outcome and wasn't even ready yet. Also, I'd gotten tied up on the phone with Trina. She had called earlier to check on me, and we had wound up spending thirty minutes on the phone, during which she'd bragged about her and Keith's trip to New York. While it had sounded like they'd had a good time, I had to cut her off quickly. I'd told her I had to go into the bathroom to shower, but technically, I'd needed to hurry up and get dressed before Cedric got here. He was a man who didn't appreciate waiting on others.

I didn't want to get left behind, so I hurried to straighten my honey-blond hair, which was parted down the middle. With so much body, my permed hair hung almost six inches past my shoulders and flowed midway down my back. My thin brows had been arched, and very little makeup covered my flawless light skin. I wore a sleeveless money-green dress that hugged my hourglass figure. It was made of linen and was cut slightly above my knees. A white cropped jacket really set my outfit off, but not as much as my gold high heels, which matched my accessories. I refused to go in front of Bryson's parents looking like a broke trick. That was what they probably expected. I had to represent, and when I looked at myself in the mirror, I was 110 percent pleased.

Right after I slid some shimmery nude gloss on my lips, I heard a light knock at the door. There was a time when Cedric had a key to let himself in, but times had surely changed. He would never get another key to my place, especially since he had put his hands on me before. He'd hit me in my mouth, causing my teeth to crack. That wasn't a good look for me, and I had had to sell a couple pairs of my red-bottom shoes to get my teeth fixed. I'd been so upset with him that day, and I had vowed never to deal with him again. But he was in a position to help me now, so I rolled with it.

When I opened the door and saw Cedric standing on the other side, I had a slight change of heart. Giving him another key could, indeed, be possible. He rocked a casual pair of black jeans that had that satisfying dick of his looking scrumptious and sitting pretty. A black leather jacket covered the deep blue button-down shirt he wore, and his Caesar cut was flowing with hella waves. His Hershey's chocolate skin was smooth, and I had to confess that he looked good enough to eat. He checked me out, too, before coming inside and asking if I was ready.

"Ready as I'll ever be," I said. "All I need to do is go to my bedroom and get my purse."

I pivoted and made my way to the bedroom. My hips purposely swayed from side to side. I was positive that my ass was doing all that it needed to do, and that Cedric wouldn't be able to resist checking it out. I wasn't exactly sure if he and Kayla were still intimate with each other or not, even though they were now divorced. But I would be sure to inquire about it the next time she and I spoke. Then again, maybe I needed to stanch these little feelings for Cedric and back off. I was just feeling a little horny, and the more I thought about it, the more I realized that nothing excited me about having sex with a man who had been shot up. He probably had numerous yucky bullet holes in his body, and from what I had heard, Paula Daniels had done some major damage to him. I had to see Cedric with all his clothes off before I made a decision to go there with him again.

After I got my purse, we left my place and headed to Cedric's car. He politely opened the passenger door for me, and the second I got inside, I got a whiff of his brand-new Audi. The leather seat hugged my body like a glove, and as he drove us to our destination, I almost fell asleep. That could have also been due to our boring time in the car. Our conversation was sporadic, until he asked if I'd had an opportunity to ask Kayla if she'd been keeping any secrets from him.

"No, I haven't had a chance to go there with her yet. We've spoken only twice since I've been home. She called to check on me, and then she called while she was at the grocery store and asked if I needed anything. She stopped by that day to drop off some of the things I requested, but she was in a rush. Said she had to pick up Jacoby from somewhere."

Cedric nodded while looking straight ahead, as if he were in deep thought. His grip on the steering wheel got tighter, and after he stopped at a red light, he turned to look at me.

"That's cool and everything, but hurry up and see what you can find out for me," he said. "I need something solid soon. I know you've been concerned about taking care of this shit with Bryson, but please don't forget about our agreement."

"I promise you that I won't forget. You have come through for me in a major way, and I owe you big-time. I will find out what I can, but I don't want to be so obvious. Kayla and I just started talking again. It may be a minute before she trusts me again. Just be patient, okay?"

The light turned green. Cedric drove off and spoke in a commanding tone. "I don't mind being patient, but after today you need to step it up a little. I need to know what's been going on behind my back. Just the other day, Kayla and Jacoby were whispering about something. I pulled her aside, inquired about it, but she said it was nothing. She was real nervous, and he's the same way when I come around. I also can't get the thoughts of her breaking into my house out of my mind. She was looking for something that day. What? I don't know yet, but I do know that you have a better chance of finding out what she was looking for than me."

Something wasn't quite adding up for me. Cedric was a smart man. He could easily do his own dirty work. There was more to this, and I also thought he was kind of upset that Kayla, Trina, and I were friends again. He couldn't stand it, and there was a possibility that he would do whatever he thought was necessary to destroy our friendship. That, to me, was obvious, and it could very well be his motive for getting me involved in this current scheme.

Several minutes later Cedric pulled into an arched driveway that accommodated at least twenty cars. The ranch-style home to my right was breathtaking. It sat on acres and acres of well-manicured land. An Olympic-sized pool to the right could be seen from afar. I was in awe as my eyes scanned the property, which was located in Wildwood, Missouri. Several miles outside of St. Louis, this city was known for housing some of the area's wealthier people, as well as celebrities. Cedric's house and Kayla's new condo weren't too far away. Kayla had definitely become a winner after their divorce, but not at the level of this. Keith and Bryson's parents had it going on, without a doubt.

"Close your mouth," Cedric said, looking in the rear-view mirror while brushing his waves. "Act like you've been to a place like this before, and remain calm, no matter what. I told them I was your uncle, and I'm here with you because I'm concerned about Bryson hurting you again. I can assure you that they don't want to see this mess play out in a courtroom, so they will throw some money on the table. Whatever their offer is, I want thirty percent for my troubles."

I tossed my head back, then let out a soft "Tuh." He was already filthy rich. What good was 30 percent going to do him?

"Thirty percent, Cedric? Really? You know that I've been suffering financially for quite some time. I barely have enough money to pay my bills, and you know that hospital bill isn't going to be cheap. Not to mention that I don't even have a job. I need every dime I can get. I don't know how much they will offer me, or if they will offer me anything at all. We don't know what kind of people we're dealing with, but agreeing to give you thirty percent may not work for me."

He shrugged, as if he didn't give a damn about anything I'd said. "Thirty percent, or I walk. Right here. Right now. I'll blow this deal wide open and let you go to court with a cheap, inexperienced lawyer and try to settle this. The choice is yours."

I sat thinking about what other choice I had. Cedric was a dirty muthafucka, and he'd taken greed to a new level. I finally responded by opening the door and getting out of the car. I guessed he figured that we had a deal, because he climbed out of the car and then walked to the front door with me, displaying a crooked smile on his face.

I reached out and rang the doorbell. Seconds later a prissy black woman with long salt-and-pepper braids answered the door. She wore an African caftan dress that flowed past her ankles, almost touching the floor. Sandals were on her feet, and her sweet perfume blew right outside the door. There was no smile whatsoever on her face, but she extended her hand to me first.

"My name is Netta," she said. "My husband and son are in the great room, waiting for you."

For the first time in a long time, I felt a little nervous. I shook her hand, then introduced myself, as well. Cedric followed suit. As we entered the house, I couldn't believe my eyes. The ceilings were roughly twelve feet tall, and that didn't include the great room ceiling, which was almost double. Swirling tan and white marble covered the floors, and someone's initials had been inscribed in the foyer in gold. The curved double staircases in the foyer were black and gold, and the crystal chandelier set everything off. The gallery was filled with black-and-white pictures of their family. Keith and Bryson appeared to be their only children, but there were also pictures of a little girl too.

The oversize bay windows in the far back lit up the whole place, and when I turned my head to the left, I could see a luxury kitchen with not one, but two granite-topped islands. This place was sick! It was in Trina's best interests to somehow or someway become a part of this family, and to do so very soon by marrying Keith. If Trina didn't already know it, she had hit the damn jackpot. I just didn't understand why she and Kayla were always so lucky. I had never been lucky enough to find a single man or one with wealthy parents whom I could benefit from.

Cedric and I followed Netta into the great room, where Bryson and his father were sitting. They stood as we entered, and all I could say to myself was, *Lord, have mercy on me*. Daddy was fine as fuck. It was no secret where Bryson and Keith had gotten their good looks from. I loved a dark-skinned man, especially one with a goatee that suited his chin and had a hint of gray in it, as did his wavy hair. His build was slim, but he was fit. His slacks fit him just right, and the silk shirt he rocked looked as if it had cost a fortune. I didn't even want to talk about the numerous diamond rings on his fingers. Was he some kind of king or something? He was tall, but just a little shorter than Bryson, who towered over all of us. There was a mean-ass mug on his face, and he looked at me as if he wanted to tear me apart. I ignored him.

Netta turned to introduce us. "Charles," she said, speaking to her husband, "this is Evelyn and her uncle, Cedric."

Charles politely extended his hand to me. When we shook hands, his soft touch sent chills up my spine. I was too ashamed to admit what effect it had on my pussy.

"Nice to meet you," he said. "Have a seat. Please."

He shook Cedric's hand too, and then we both sat in white plush chairs that looked as if they had just been purchased yesterday. Everything was so tidy, spotless, and clean. I hoped that the juices leaking from my pussy wouldn't ruin the chair, but looking at ole Charles just did something to me.

Charles sat on a sofa on the opposite side of the room, next to Bryson, while Netta made her way to another room.

"I'll be back with some drinks," she said. "Go ahead and carry on without me."

Drinks? I didn't think it was that kind of occasion. I also didn't know if that bitch would try to poison me, so there would be no drinking for me.

Charles rubbed his hands together while looking directly at me. "I'm glad your uncle reached out to us about discussing this little situation. Bryson has already informed us of his side of the story. My wife and I would like to hear yours."

Bryson placed his hands behind his head and pursed his lips. He then yawned, as if it was a waste of his time to be here. The smug look on his face irritated me. I hated to be in his presence, though the only thing it took me back to was the day I saw him getting screwed by that tranny, and the day he came to my apartment to hurt me. Nonetheless, I appeared relaxed and started to answer Charles.

"I'm not exactly sure what Bryson told you about what happened, but I'll start by saying that my encounter with him was one of the worst experiences of my life. I thought I was going to die, and there is nothing that a woman could ever do to a man to deserve a beating like the one I got."

Netta came back into the room, carrying several drinks on a tray. After she placed the tray on a table, she took a seat in a chair to listen in. I described what had happened, starting from the moment Bryson banged on my door, then kicked it down to get inside my apartment. I wasn't even sure if that was how it happened, but I made sure that what I told them was more dramatic than ever. Everyone was tuned in, and it wasn't long before disgust washed across Charles's face. Netta kept nodding her head, and there were a few shrugs here and there. As for Bryson, he kept biting down on his lip. His fists tightened at one point; then he released them and wiggled his fingers.

Tears rushed to the rims of my eyes as I spoke about how he had had his hands wrapped around my neck and how I had been unable to breathe. "He was too strong for me, and there was nothing that I could do to get him off of me. My vision was blurred, and after he removed his hands from my neck, all I could see were his fists pounding me over and over again in my face. My whole body felt numb. I—I kept choking on a bunch of blood that had filled my mouth. My head hurt so badly, and he was yanking my hair and beating me in the head at the same time. I didn't—"

Bryson slammed his fist down on the table in front of him. "Stop fucking lying, bitch!" he shouted. Spit flew from his mouth, as he was unable to contain himself. "You know it didn't go down like that, and if I had wanted you dead, trust me, you would be."

Charles's face twisted, and there were numerous thick wrinkles visible on his forehead. "Calm the hell down!" he yelled. "Don't you ever speak that way in front of your mother and me! And the last time I checked, we do have guests."

Bryson cut his eyes, then looked over at his mother, who was shaking her head. She didn't say a word. I was ready to continue, but Charles sent me in another direction.

"What brought all of this about, Evelyn? What did you do to him, or what did he do to you, other than beat you up? Something had to bring the two of you to that point."

Well, he asked, and I had already prepared an answer. I looked at Bryson's mother first. There was a chance that she might not want to hear this. It was obvious that Bryson was a mama's boy, and the last thing I wanted to do was hurt her little feelings.

"Miss Netta," I said as politely as I could, "I don't know if you want to stay in the room to hear this, but I came here to speak nothing but the truth."

"Then go ahead and speak your so-called truth," she said with a slight attitude. "We're all listening."

I figured that ole cockeyed bitch didn't believe me. No matter what I said, she was Team Bryson. I ignored her comment about me telling the so-called truth, and I kept my eyes on Charles. Bryson was in my sights too. The look in his eyes dared me to tell his parents that I had caught him getting dicked down by a man. I guessed he didn't think I would go into details, but I was prepared to.

"First, let me say that I have nothing against gay people," I stated. "My best friend, Trina, is bisexual, and I love her to death. With that being said, Bryson lied to me. He made me believe that he was straight. Did all kinds of things to me sexually, and the things I did to him I'm too embarrassed to say in front of my uncle. Had Bryson just been honest with me about his sexual preferences, we wouldn't even be here."

Bryson jumped up and darted his finger at me. "Bitch, I will hurt you for lying on me! What in the hell is wrong with you? Wasn't that beat down I gave you enough? You can't come into my parents' home and lie on me like this!"

He charged forward, but Charles stood and held him back. That was when Cedric stood up to protect me. I was surprised by his swift actions.

"None of that, so chill!" Cedric said to Bryson. "You've already hurt her enough, and you will not do it again."

"Man, fuck you! She's a goddamned liar! You don't even know the half of it!"

"Sit down!" Charles shouted at Bryson. "Or get out of here. I thought you'd be able to handle yourself better than this, but I see you're having some problems controlling yourself."

"It's hard to sit here and allow somebody to lie on me like this," Bryson muttered. "If you want to talk to me when she leaves, fine. I'm out."

Bryson stormed away. It was no surprise when his mother went after him.

"Sweetheart," she said, trailing behind him, "everything is going to be fine. Calm down, and don't you leave this house just yet. Go downstairs and cool off for a while. Your dad and I will handle this, okay?"

Bryson did exactly as his mommy had told him to. Babying a grown-ass man would do him no good. No wonder he wasn't about shit.

After he went downstairs to cool off, Netta returned to the great room. Charles and Cedric sat back down, and I was asked to continue.

I wiped a slow tear that was sliding down my face. "I never meant to hurt anyone, and the truth is, I had some very deep feelings for Bryson. By not telling me his status, he didn't give me a choice. I was upset about it, and I didn't know anything until I caught him having sex with a transgender man. I told my best friend about it, and that's when all hell broke loose. Bryson went on a rampage. He was determined to kill me."

"You can stop right there," Netta said, holding up her hand. "I don't believe a word you're saying, and shame on you for spreading vicious lies. You mentioned that your best friend, Trina, is bisexual, but isn't she the one who is dating my son Keith? If so, I met Trina before. We speak quite often, and I know for a fact that she loves Keith and only Keith."

Shit. Shit. Shit. I had totally forgotten about Trina being with Keith. In no way had I intended to mention her name or her past. I hoped like hell that this wouldn't get back to her. If it did, I knew that she was going to be very upset with me. I attempted to clear things up, but doing so made me look like a for-real liar, when in reality, I wasn't lying.

"Trina is my best friend, but a long time ago she expressed to me that she had a thing for women. I'm not sure if she was serious or not, but this isn't about Trina. It's about Bryson. Whether you want to believe me or not, your son needs to fess up and accept who he really is. His lies are going to hurt many more people, and from what I already know, he has already hurt plenty of the women he's dated."

Netta stood, then looked at Charles. "I've heard enough. You can do what you want to about this, but I'm not going to sit here and listen to all this craziness about my son." She looked at me with the evilest gaze I had ever seen. Her pupils grew bigger, and then her eyes narrowed. "You are one deceitful woman. I'm getting all kinds of negative vibes from you. Hurry up and finish with your lies, and then get the hell out of here before the devil in you causes this house to burn to the ground."

She walked off, leaving all of us stunned, even Charles, who sat wringing his hands together and looking down at the floor, as if he were in deep thought.

"I understand how your wife feels," Cedric said, trying to get back to the business at hand. "She wants to protect her son. I want to protect my niece too, so what are we going to do about this situation? Do we want a jury to decide who was in the wrong? Or can we settle this once and for all right now?"

Charles looked up. He stared at me and Cedric with his light brown eyes, which resembled Bryson's. He released a deep sigh, then sat back on the sofa with his hands behind his head.

"I love my son, and I am well aware that he has some issues. Issues that I don't want to discuss with the two of you, but I will say, Evelyn, that I don't believe everything you've sat there and told me today. I am, however, prepared to make you some kind of peace offering that will make this all go away today. And after today, we don't want to hear anything else about it. A gag order will be included in our agreement, and if any word of this gets out, there will be major consequences. So, the next questions are, how much and can we make a deal?"

His words were like music to my ears. I had already thought about how much, and when I blurted it out, Cedric coughed, then cleared his throat.

"My niece is probably still feeling the effects of that beat down she got, because her head couldn't be on straight if she's requesting that kind of settlement. Add two more zeros to that amount for pain and lifetime suffering, and, we, sir, have a deal."

Okay. Maybe I did short myself a little. It wasn't until then that I realized just how important and helpful Cedric being here was.

Charles kept nodding his head, and then he stood up and extended his hand to me. "Deal," he said, waiting for me to accept.

I stood and happily extended my hand to his. "Yes. We have ourselves a deal."

Charles said he needed to call his attorney and would be right back. Within the next hour or so, I was asked to read over an agreement that would set me up pretty for the rest of my life. Needless to say, I was ecstatic. I thanked Charles before I left by wrapping my arms around his neck and pressing my breasts against his chest.

“I’m glad we could work this out,” I said. “I thank you for doing the right thing, and please tell your wife that I thank her for her time, as well.”

Charles patted my back, then backed away from the tight embrace. Cedric damn near had to pull me out the door to get me away from Charles. And when we got in the car, he chewed me out.

“Is that all you think about? Some goddamned dick? You almost blew it in there, and that woman wasn’t playing with you, Evelyn. She looked like she was about to cut your fucking throat. I’m warning you. If that pussy of yours can’t control itself, you’d better figure out a way to shut that shit down and stay the hell away from her husband.”

I rolled my eyes at Cedric, even though he knew me all too well. Charles was on my hit list, and I didn’t give two cents about his wife. For now, though, I had something else to be excited about.

“Forget all that mess you’re talking about right now. I am rich! Did you hear what I said? I. Am. Rich! All I’m thinking about is shopping. Ole Netta can keep Charles, but she’d better hope like hell that I never come face-to-face with him again and she’s not around. If not, I will fuck his brains out and send him back to her with my pussy juices all over his lips. Just like I may decide to send you back to your lover tonight. I’m in the mood to celebrate my new fortune.”

I playfully placed my hand on his lap, but he quickly removed it.

“I don’t know how to say this to you, but hell, fucking, no. You couldn’t pay me to tamper with that coochie again, and quite frankly, I’ve already had enough of it.”

We laughed, but Cedric quickly changed his mind after I lowered my head to his lap and damn near sucked the skin off his dick. It always tasted so good to me, and he could never resist my head game.

We arrived at my place several minutes later. He damn near broke the door down to get inside and have sex with me. I was so sure that Kayla wouldn't approve of this, but little did she know that Cedric just didn't move me the way he used to. As he lay on top of me, I stared at the ceiling, wondering how I was going to get rid of him.

2

Trina

I was exhausted from my trip to New York with Keith. We had attended an art expo, and it had let me know I had major work to do if I wanted to get serious about my art career. I'd seen artwork from some of the most famous artists in the world. Pieces that had me in awe and that I couldn't get off my mind. Some of Keith's work was comparable, but even he too felt as if his work wasn't up to par. He had discovered his gift when he was in his teens. His parents had sent him to some of the best art schools to learn more, and he worked almost every single day to perfect his skills. I, on the other hand, saw it as a hobby and a way to make a little cash here and there. That was until my trip to New York. I had realized how much love I had for art, so I intended to indulge myself much more, as well as to step it up on my interior decorating. I used to go that route, as well, but not so much lately.

While Keith was upstairs in the studio, I was in the kitchen, cooking breakfast. Things between us had been only okay, simply because Keith had been worried about the situation between Evelyn and Bryson. I had found myself caught in the middle. Evelyn was my friend; Keith was my man. I knew Bryson was guilty of doing what he'd done to her, and he continued to lie about what Evelyn had said when she caught him with another man. Just the other day, Keith and I had got into another disagreement about Bryson putting his hands on her. I couldn't believe that Keith condoned it and that he'd said that Evelyn deserved everything she got. I had a problem with that because I had seen her in that hospital bed, clinging to life. No one deserved that. The bottom line was Bryson needed to come clean.

We had gotten to the point where I didn't want Bryson over here and Keith didn't want Evelyn here. Keith had every right to be angry with her for trying to get him in bed with her, but that issue had been resolved. I had handled it, and Evelyn now knew that Keith was mine and only mine. She had apologized for what she had done, and even though a part of me still did not completely trust her, I was glad that we all considered ourselves friends again.

Mending our friendship had taken work. Faced with this work, most people would have said, "To hell with it." I had had a lot of convincing to do with Kayla, and we both had had to dig deep in order to forgive Evelyn. I thought about how I would have felt if she had died that day. If Bryson had killed her, how would I have handled it? We all had had unresolved issues, and I would have felt horrible for not working things out with her. We had been friends for too long. There had been ups, as well as downs. But thankfully, we had been able to focus on the true meaning of forgiveness and had pulled it all together and had remained friends.

I was just about done with preparing breakfast when I heard my cell phone ringing. It was on the kitchen table, so I walked away from the stove and went to answer it. I didn't recognize the number, but the voice sounded familiar.

"It's me, Sasha Bolden. One of the artists you met while in New York. You gave me your number to call you. Remember?"

I snapped my fingers, then smiled. "Yes. I remember now. How are you?"

"I'm doing well. Thanks for asking. I'm glad you made it home safely, and I wondered if you gave more thought to what I mentioned to you while you were here."

In New York Keith and I had been in an art class together, learning new things, and there we'd met Sasha. I had mentioned to her that I originally saw my art as a hobby, but after observing a portrait I'd done, she'd felt that I had major potential, and she'd encouraged me to do more. She'd insisted that she could help me. She'd also said that she could get my paintings in front of some serious art buyers and help me make money. I'd told Keith about it, but he hadn't seem as enthused about it as I was. New York was definitely a place where I could make a lot of money if I wanted to, but I wasn't up to traveling there more than once or twice a year. Sasha had mentioned that I should travel there more to showcase my work.

"I've given it some thought," I said. "But I'm not sure what I really want to do yet."

"Would that be because of Keith? If so, let me say this to you. You can't let anyone hold you back. If you have an opportunity to get your work out there more, jump on it. I can help you out a lot. Just give it some more thought and then let me know what you decide."

"I'm not letting anyone hold me back. If I believe this is going to be a good opportunity for me, I will definitely jump on it. I need time to think about it, though. I'll let you know something soon, and thanks for calling me."

We ended the call on that note. I stood there in thought while tapping the phone against the palm of my hand. I was confused about what to do, but I sure as hell didn't want to turn away money or mess up an opportunity to become a well-known artist. There was also something else that weighed heavily on my mind. I was a little bit attracted to Sasha. She was a beautiful black woman who was very likable, hilarious, and fun to be around. Her natural fro was beautiful, and her curves weren't nothing to play with. I could tell she worked out a lot, like I did, and I appreciated how knowledgeable she was about art. She had spent a lot of time with me and Keith while we were in New York. I liked her style, and I'd been a little sad when we all parted ways. I wondered if Keith had seen me checking her out. Had he noticed lust in my eyes? I was glad that she lived in New York and I was miles and miles away in St. Louis. If she lived here, God help me. I would probably be at her doorstep right now, trying to see what these feelings would lead to.

The crazy thing was, I thought that I was done with women, especially after what had happened between me and crazy-ass Lexi. After she wound up trying to kill Keith, I had promised myself that I would never lie to him again about my feelings. But there I was again, holding back on how I felt inside. I guessed it wasn't a biggie, and I didn't think it was necessary to mention a simple crush. The bottom line was, I loved Keith to death. And one day I intended to be his wife.

As I entered the upstairs studio with a breakfast tray in my hands, I could see Keith sitting behind a tall canvas. His legs straddled a stool, and with his shirt off, the numerous tattoos covering his biceps were on display. I had myself one of the sexiest men in the world. I could kick myself for thinking about being with another woman, but seeing him in his boxers surely made my thoughts switch gears. I stepped forward, and the second he saw me with the tray in my hands, a wide smile appeared on his face. His pearly whites showed, and he reached out for my waist. I placed the tray on the floor, then sat on his lap.

"You are so sweet," he said. "But if you plan on interrupting me, you'd better make sure you're bringing me more than just breakfast."

"I'm bringing you breakfast and then some. Take whatever you wish. . . . I'm all yours."

Keith planted a soft kiss on my shoulder, then reached for the glass of orange juice on the tray. As he took a sip, I looked at the painting he'd been working on since we'd gotten back from our trip. It was an abstract design that displayed numerous bright colors. I loved it.

"Your painting is coming along well. I'm feeling the abstract look of this, and it's good to see you venture away from what you normally do," I remarked.

"I'm trying," he said. "New York was a wake-up call for me, and if I want to compete, I have to do much better."

"Me too. You know I've been thinking about stepping up my game too. After the call I got today from Sasha, I think I may let her help me out. I'll see what she can do to get me to the next level."

Keith shot down my comment real quick. "I doubt that she'll be able to help you, Trina, so don't get your hopes up too high. People are always talking about what they can do to help your career, and most of the time, all it is a bunch of talk. I sensed that from her. If you ask me, she talks too damn much."

I was surprised by Keith's response, but he'd been this way lately. Kind of on edge a little and real blunt about certain things.

"I get that some people make promises that they can't keep, but I have a feeling that she's genuine."

"Genuine? No, I wasn't feeling a genuine person when she was around. As a matter of fact, the word *genuine* was far from what I felt."

I released a deep sigh, then continued. "I'm not sure what you're sensing about her, but whatever it is, you didn't seem that way while we were in New York. You were talking just as much as she was, and the two of you seemed to get along just fine."

"I know how to handle myself when it comes to business, but I didn't go to New York to make new friends. I just don't want to see you get your hopes up too high, and maybe you should focus more on trying to enhance your skills first."

Keith had always believed that he was more talented than I was. Whether that was true or not, I didn't like where we were going with this conversation.

"I do need to improve my work, but so do you. And when all is said and done, if I can get paid for my work, I will."

I stood, only for Keith to pull me back down on his lap. "Listen," he said. "I'm not trying to insult your work or anything like that, okay? There's just something about that Sasha chick that didn't sit right with me. She seemed very nosy. And I didn't know that you had given her your phone number."

"I gave it to her because she said she could help me. I didn't get the same vibes from her as you did, but if I ever sense that something isn't right with her, you know I'll back off."

"Just like you did with Evelyn, huh? She hasn't been out of the hospital for two weeks, and she's already causing trouble."

A frown covered my face. I surely didn't know how we'd got from Sasha to Evelyn. It seemed like Keith was purposely trying to kick up an argument with me.

"How is Evelyn causing trouble? What has she done now?"

"I'll let her tell you all about it. I'm sure she will, but then again, maybe she won't remember to tell you that she told my parents you were bisexual."

"What?" I shouted. "When . . .? Why would she tell your parents that?"

"She met with them to discuss that situation with Bryson. During their conversation, she felt that it was necessary to mention that you were bisexual. My mother called me, and so did Bryson. I've had it with your conniving-ass BFF, and I wish you would wake up when it comes to her. She is trouble. When will you and Kayla ever learn?"

I was shocked that Evelyn would bring up my name while talking to Keith's parents. What in the hell was she up to now? I couldn't wait to call her, but for now, I had to find out what Keith's response was to his parents.

"I will deal with Evelyn later, but what did you tell your mother?"

"I told her the truth. I don't want you to ever feel as if you have to cover up who you are, and I'm not ashamed of the woman I fell in love with."

His answer put a smile on my face. I was so lucky to have a man like Keith in my corner.

"I love you too, and thanks for keeping it real with her. Did she say anything after that?"

"She did, but I don't want to talk about it right now. What I want to do is eat breakfast before it gets cold and get busy again with painting. I also want to go to the fitness center to work out, but only after we get a little workout here first."

"Count me in, as always."

We ate breakfast, scratched sex for now, and then changed to go to the gym. I couldn't stop thinking about what Keith's mother now thought about me. Some people had no love for individuals like me, and even though Bryson was who he was, his mother didn't seem like she was the type who would embrace something like this with open arms. If she ever asked me what the deal was, I wouldn't deny it. And if her feelings about me had changed, so be it.

Meanwhile, I was highly upset with Evelyn for putting my business out there. While Keith was upstairs, putting on his tennis shoes, I went downstairs to call her. She answered the phone, sounding as upbeat as ever.

"It's funny that you called," she said. "I was just at Foot Locker, trying to decide what size shoe you wear. I saw these cute tennis shoes that have your name written all over them. They're only eighty bucks, and they're green, gray, and navy. Are you still a size eight, or have your feet grown?"

"I wear a size nine, but aside from the tennis shoes, can I ask you a question?"

"Sure. What's on your mind?"

"Why did you tell Keith's parents I was bisexual? That's none of their business. If I wanted them to know, I would have told them myself."

"I get that, but the truth is, it slipped. I didn't mean to say anything about you, but as I was talking to them about Bryson accepting who he is, I accidentally mentioned your name. I apologize, but at the same time, if you were or if you still are bisexual, I don't want you to be ashamed of it. You kept your secret long enough, and to hell with Keith's parents if they don't approve. That mother of his is a real bitch. I don't see how you've been able to get along with a woman like that."

Evelyn was trying to change the subject, but she was right about his parents. To hell with their feelings about me.

"I'm not ashamed of who I am, but that doesn't mean that you have to spread my business to the whole world. Keith's mother and I get along very well, so please don't refer to her as a bitch. You must have done or said something to her that really pissed her off. You also never told me that you were planning to meet with them about your situation with Bryson. How did that turn out?"

"All I can say is well," Evelyn replied. "It turned out very well, and everything worked out for the best. I can't say much more than that, because of a gag order, but I'm sure Keith will provide you with more details."

"I'm sure he will too. Meanwhile, get back to whatever you were doing, and we'll chat later. Glad you're feeling better."

"Much better. And when you have time, I want to take you and Kayla to dinner. It's the least I can do, so let me know what you're up to this Sunday. I know church isn't on your agenda, but maybe some time after two or three will work."

"Why are you over there trying to throw shade? Church isn't on my agenda, and I'm sure it's not on yours, either, you sinner. "

Evelyn laughed. "Aren't we all? But you're right. It's not on my agenda. But I serve the same God as you. He's sho' 'nough been good to me, and I'm thankful for my new blessings."

I didn't bother to reply about her new blessings. Evelyn had things twisted. It was obvious that she'd managed to swindle some money out of Keith's parents. I wanted to know how much, so on the way to the gym with Keith, I asked him if he knew.

"I know, but I'm not supposed to talk about it. I'm so angry about the whole thing, and I'm sick and tired of my parents bailing Bryson out of these situations. We made up after the fight, but certain things will never be forgotten. I don't like how he treated you, and he has no respect for our parents."

"I know how you feel about him. I feel the same way about Evelyn. She has a big mouth, and I told her that I didn't appreciate her telling your parents about me. But it is what it is. I just hope that they don't look at me differently now."

Keith didn't respond.

I was sure he was holding back on what his mother now thought of me, but the past was the past. I couldn't do anything to change who I was, but I was worried about speaking of my sexual desires for women as if they no longer existed. There was something stirring inside of me again. First, there were my surprising feelings for Sasha. And when we got to the gym, I jogged on the treadmill and observed a woman's nice, heart-shaped ass in front of me. Keith jogged beside me, and even though I'd seen him take a quick glance at her butt, my eyes were glued to it more than his were. I tried to play it off by watching the TV mounted on the wall, but my eyes kept traveling back to the same place—her ass. Dirty thoughts swam in my head, and I visualized her ass cheeks spread across my face. I was so disturbed by what I was feeling that I stopped the treadmill to go cool off.

"Where are you going?" Keith asked, still jogging. I looked at the sweat dripping from his sexy body, and all I could think was, *Shame on me*.

"I need some water. I also want to work with the weights, so I'll be over there."

"Give me twenty or so more minutes on the treadmill and I'll join you."

He continued his workout on the treadmill, while I moved on over to the weights. I kept taking peeks at the beautiful woman, and when she got off the treadmill, I saw her walk over to a man who was doing sit-ups on a mat. They kissed, and a few minutes later they left together. Out of sight, out of mind. I was left thinking about my relationship with Keith. I certainly didn't want to lose him, but how long would I be able to curb my desires?

3

Kayla

I seriously thought I'd gotten rid of my problem. After divorcing Cedric, I had figured my little world would be peachy keen. But now I had a bigger issue to deal with—drinking too much alcohol. It had started off as a casual thing. Then I had found myself drinking just to take away the pain. The pain had never really gone away, especially since this thing with Jacoby reaching out to Paula Daniels for her to kill Cedric was still fresh in my head. I wished like hell that she hadn't followed through with the plan. Jacoby said he had tried to stop her from shooting Cedric, but by then her mind had been made up and she'd been too far gone. I was on edge every time Cedric stopped by. He kept questioning me about my demeanor, but I didn't have the guts or the courage to tell him that Jacoby had been involved in planning his demise.

As for Jacoby, he seemed to be doing much better than I was. But there was no doubt that he was just as worried as I was about Cedric finding out the truth. We knew what kind of damage Cedric could do if he ever found out, and there was no question in my mind that he would have Jacoby arrested. In no way could I see my son in jail. He wasn't that kind of kid, and he didn't deserve to be put behind bars. The other prisoners would eat him alive, and it made me sick to my stomach when I thought about my baby being in a place like that. At the end of the day, I viewed this as being my fault. Had I handled my business with Cedric a long time ago and divorced him when he first cheated on me, we wouldn't be in this predicament right now. But for many years, I had held on for the wrong reasons. I'd caused my son more damage than I'd realized. He'd felt as if he didn't have a choice, and I totally understood why he'd wanted Cedric dead.

Jacoby had felt that I was weak and that he needed to stand up for me. Now I had to stand up for him too. If I had to lie and say that I was the one who had put him up to it, I would. I would go that far and do jail time. I was prepared for wherever the chips fell, but meanwhile, I needed something to help calm my nerves and enable me to cope with all that was unfolding around me. For now, alcohol was, indeed, my best friend. I was afraid to talk to Trina or Evelyn about my problems, and I did my best to keep up a good front. They both thought that from the outside looking in, my life was still perfect, even without Cedric. I had money to do whatever, a son who loved me to death, an ex who now respected me, and two friends who were as close to me as sisters. After all that had happened, they were still like sisters to me. Evelyn had turned over a new leaf, and maybe it had taken her being on her deathbed to realize her mistakes. We all got those wake-up calls. It seemed as if hers had come right on time.

While Jacoby was at the mall with his girlfriend, Adrianne, I was at home, watching TV. My new condo was decked out, and I had recently hired an interior decorator to hook up my kitchen and hearth room. She had jazzed it up with a new color palette: olive green, tan, and white. My flat-screen TV hung above a wall-mounted fireplace, and an array of beautiful art covered the walls. All my furniture was traditional, and I was very particular about people coming over and putting their shoes on my sofas, especially Evelyn, who disrespected my place no matter where I lived. In the past, if she wasn't somewhere in my home fucking Cedric, she was somewhere with her feet propped up on my furniture or with a lit cigarette. I had called her out on that mess too, and it was good to know that we were now on the same page.

She had called earlier to tell me she had something for me and was on her way over. I hadn't seen her since I left her place the other day, and I didn't mind her coming over. I was bored and needed someone to talk to. And with her being here, I wouldn't think about drinking so much. It seemed like whenever I was alone, alcohol was the only thing on my mind.

With an empty glass in my hand, I looked at the clock on the wall. It was a little after two in the afternoon, and there I was, still in my pajamas. I figured I'd better go into my bedroom and put on some clothes, so I stood to go do just that. As I walked past the bar, I looked at the almost empty bottle of vodka. There was only a little swig left, so I decided to get another glass and finish it off. After pouring it, I tossed the liquid down my throat, then swallowed hard. My eyes watered from the burning sensation in my throat—a feeling that I had gotten used to. I felt a little more upbeat, so I turned on some music, which played throughout my condo, and listened to Jill Scott break it all down for me.

While singing along, I changed into a pair of tight jeans and a ribbed tank top that revealed my tiny nipples. I wasn't in the mood for a bra, nor was I in the mood to put on any makeup. My dark skin was flawless, and I loved the way my short hair had grown on me. I kept it cut low and lined to perfection. Cedric hadn't had anything nice to say to me when I first got it cut, but he had later admitted that it was the best thing I could have done to show off my round face and doe eyes. I appreciated his compliments more than he knew, especially since he had barely had anything nice to say to me when we were married. I had never thought we'd be able to get along as we did, but I guessed it was like that because we were no longer under the same roof.

As soon as I closed the blinds in my bedroom, the doorbell rang. I made my way to the door, thinking that it was Evelyn. Instead, it was Cedric. His pop-up visits annoyed me a little. Since his office and his new home were close by, he often stopped by to check on me and Jacoby. While Cedric was not Jacoby's biological father, he still considered Jacoby his son.

I opened the door with a fake smile on my face. "It would be nice for you to call before coming over, Cedric. We're not here all the time, and I would hate for you to waste gas."

He walked inside, bringing the smell of Clive Christian cologne with him. His tailored suit was always on point, and as usual, his waves were flowing.

"I came to see what Jacoby was getting into this weekend. He's been dodging me, and we've never gone this long without spending some father-and-son time together. Every time I suggest that we go somewhere, he comes up with excuses. Haven't you noticed?"

I closed the door, then made my way toward the kitchen. Cedric followed.

"No, I haven't noticed. But he's a teenager, Cedric. I'm sure he doesn't want to be doing things with you all the time. Besides, Adrianne keeps him quite busy. He spends a lot of his free time with her."

"I get that, but I also know that he's been avoiding me. And it's not like I'm trying to just hang out with him anywhere. What teenager wouldn't want to go to an NBA championship game? Who would turn down going to

Dubai or taking a trip to Hawaii? I even suggested that he bring Adrianne along, and he still made excuses. I know that finding out I wasn't his real father upset him, but at the end of the day, I'm the one who raised him."

Cedric was making this more difficult than it needed to be. He needed to back off and give Jacoby some space. "You can't force him to do what he doesn't want to do. And to be honest with you, I think that he's been struggling with this whole father thing. You and I did a lot of damage to him. I'm not sure if he's completely over it."

Cedric opened the fridge, then removed a bottle of water. He unscrewed the cap, then looked at me. "Correction. You did a lot of damage by not telling either of us the truth. Don't put me in that mess, and please take responsibility for your actions."

I rolled my eyes. He didn't have to go there, did he? Yes, I had messed up by not telling Jacoby the truth about his real father, Arnez, but I wasn't going to beat myself up about it.

"I have taken responsibility for my actions, and I'm going to encourage you to do the same. As a matter of fact, I don't even want to talk about this right now. Jacoby is gone, and he won't be back until later."

Cedric guzzled down most of the water, then placed the bottle on the island. He licked across his lips to moisten them.

"I guess I'll call him later to see what's up, but I'm sure I'm going to get the same ole song and dance. As for you, what's been up? It smells like a brewery when I walk in here. And just so you know, I am paying attention. The liquid in those bottles over there is getting lower and lower by the day."

I turned my head to look at the numerous bottles on the bar. I didn't know that Cedric had been paying attention. Was the smell of alcohol really that prominent in here?

"I'm doing fine. I was vacuuming the other day, and I hit the liquor cabinet over there with the vacuum cleaner by accident. Some of the bottles hit the floor, and the liquids spilled on my carpet. I need to call a carpet cleaning company to come clean the carpet."

"You do that," he said, finishing off the water. "And while you're at it, you may want to attend a few AA meetings too. I can't believe you would try to feed me that bullshit you just said, but I can say that it doesn't surprise me. The one thing I can say is, you do always do your best to cover up a lie."

I wasn't sure what Cedric was referring to, but I tried not to make much of his comment. Either way, his words upset me. He was always coming over here, trying to run my and Jacoby's lives. He seemed to make my alcohol problem a bigger issue than it was, but I didn't know why I was surprised by that. Anything to belittle me was the name of his game.

I tried to change the subject. "Whether you want to believe it or not, I have things under control over here. What you need to worry about is your new home and the woman you now have living with you, Joy. When are the two of you getting married? She couldn't wait for us to get divorced, so I know she has already gone out and picked out her dress."

"Breaking news, baby. Marriage is not in my future again. In my eyes, women are only good for one thing and one thing only. No offense to you."

His eyes traveled to my tiny breasts, which were visible underneath my tank. I snatched the bottle of water from his hand, then tossed it in the trash can.

"I am highly offended, and I can't believe you would say something like that. If that's how you truly feel—"

Suddenly the doorbell rang.

Saved by the bell, I thought when I heard the doorbell. This time it had to be Evelyn. It had been a long time since we were all in the same room. I wondered how the two of them would react upon seeing each other. The last thing Trina had told me was that Cedric had knocked out Evelyn's teeth. I didn't want any chaos to go down today, so I warned him that that was probably her at the door.

He shrugged, then followed behind me as I made my way to the door. "I'm surprised that you're still friends with that bitch, but that's your choice. I'm getting ready to go. Tell Jacoby I'll holla later."

The second I opened the door, Evelyn's bright smile vanished. Cedric walked around me to make his way outside. He didn't say one word to Evelyn. She stood with her mouth wide open. Several bags were in her hands, and it looked as if she'd just gotten her hair done. Long curls hung past her shoulders, and the short dress and high heels she wore made her look as if she was ready to go party.

"Ugggh," she said, looking at Cedric as he walked off to his car. "What's his problem? Or should I be asking, what is he doing here? Are the two of you getting back together?"

Honestly, I didn't feel comfortable discussing Cedric with Evelyn. She didn't need to know the purpose of his visit, and if we were getting back together, she would be the last person I would tell.

"Come on in here and stop asking me questions about Cedric. I don't want to talk about that man. I'd rather talk about how you've been doing."

With a smile back on her face, Evelyn trotted into the living room with her bags. She placed them on the floor and then sat on the sofa, crossing her long legs.

"I've been doing great, but come sit by me so the two of us can talk."

I walked into the room, watching closely as Evelyn checked me out from head to toe.

"You've lost more weight," she said. "Girl, what are you trying to do? Model again?"

"No, not at all." I sat beside her. "Just been eating healthy, exercising a lot, and trying to raise my son to the best of my ability."

"Well," she said, patting my leg, "you've done a great job with Jacoby. If I had a son, I would want him to be just like him."

I smiled, but her comment made me think about her being pregnant by Cedric. I truly needed to let go of the past, but a tiny part of me couldn't.

"Okay," Evelyn said, rubbing her hands together. "I bought you some thank-you gifts, and before I give them to you, I have a few things that I want to say. First, thank you so much for being there for me when I needed you. You and Trina are truly the best, and I don't know what I would have done in that hospital without your support. I know that forgiving me wasn't easy, and if the shoe were on the other foot, I don't know if I could have done it. But you've always been a better person than me, Kayla. I'm working on myself, and I must say that I'm embracing the new me and loving all the goodness that has come my way."

This certainly seemed like a new and reformed Evelyn in front of me, but as always, it was wise not to trust everything she said. While I did believe that the whole situation between her and Bryson had changed her, it was yet to be seen if it was for the good or the bad. Either way, I reached out to give her a hug.

"Apology accepted. Now, stop trying to make me cry and tell me what's in those bags for me. I see Jimmy Choo bags on down to Michael Kors. What did I do to deserve all of this?"

We laughed, and when all was said and done, Evelyn had outdone herself. She certainly knew my taste. From the purses to the fabulous shoes to the watch, I loved it all.

"Thank you, my dear friend, but you really didn't have to do all of this. You know I'm about to ask where you got the money from, but you don't have to tell me if you don't think it's any of my business."

"Look, my business is your business. While I can't tell you how much they gave me, I will say that Bryson's parents hooked me up! They knew he was at fault, and they were willing to do whatever to make sure I didn't put their son's business out there. I'm pleased by how everything turned out, and as long as I don't ever have to ever see him again, I'm good."

"That's good. I'm glad you all were able to settle everything without going to court. Put the money they gave you to good use, and please keep much of it in a savings account. Shopping is nice, but if you don't budget your money correctly, you'll find yourself in the hole again."

"I am making smarter choices, but I had to go splurge a little on some of the things I've always wanted. I also wanted to do something nice for my BFF's, especially you. I borrowed from you until I couldn't borrow anymore. I want to pay back some of the money you gave me, and since you and Cedric aren't together anymore, I suspect that things may be a little tight around here."

I wasted no time setting the record straight. While Evelyn might have gotten a substantial amount of cash from Bryson's parents, I doubted that the money would last a lifetime. It would surprise me if she still had any money six months from now. I wasn't hating. Just being honest.

"Girl, with or without Cedric, I will be just fine. You know I wasn't about to walk away broke after our divorce, and I'm happy to say that he was willing, and able, to give me everything I asked for."

Evelyn clapped her hands. "That's wonderful. And now we must celebrate. Not only on Sunday, when I'm planning to take my BFF's to dinner, but right here and right now too."

She removed a champagne bottle from one of the bags. I went to the kitchen to get wineglasses, and within the hour, we found ourselves drunk, giggling, and delving into a conversation that I didn't want to have with her.

"I needed this," I said. "Lord knows, I needed to let go and feel free again."

I raised my arms in the air, then waved my hands like a bird.

"Fr-free?" Evelyn slurred. "Free from who or what?"

"From my past. I feel so much better, but there is one little thing that is still bugging the heck out of me." I fell back on the sofa after I took another sip of the vodka I had put on ice.

Evelyn crawled on the floor, then maneuvered her way into one of my wingback chairs. "If it has anything to do with me," she said, woozy and pointing at me, "let it all out. Don't hold back, 'cause I totally understand if you still got some problems with me."

I sat up, then waved my finger in front of me. "Noooo. Not with you, but with my ex and my son. What am I going to do about them?"

Evelyn sipped from her wineglass, then slammed it on the table in front of her. "What? Exactly what do you mean? Stop talking in riddles and spill it!"

I placed my finger over my lips, then whispered, "Shhh. If I tell you, you can't say one word about this to anyone. Not even Trinaaaaa."

"Yo . . . your secret is safe with me. Maybe not with the old Evelyn . . ." She laughed. "But definitely with the new Evelyn."

I laughed too. I smacked my leg, then laughed even louder. "Right. That old Evelyn was something else. But the new Evelyn, I'm kind of liking this bitch."

"Ooh, girl, stop. Shut yo' mouth and keep on talking. I'm listening too, bitch."

I pointed my finger at her. "Tyler Perry gon' get you for biting his stuff. But, anyway, as I was saying, Cedric and me . . . we still been screwing around from time to time."

"What?" Evelyn shouted, then sat up in the chair. "Are you telling me that you still been giving that man all your precious goodies?"

I held up one finger. "Ju-just one time, but he keeps coming over here, trying to get into my panties. I don't know if I should let him in again or not, but when I tell you that man knows how to make my juices flow, I mean he really knows how to make my juices flow. I don't know who I'm gon' find to replace him."

"Hey, you ain't talking to a woman who don't already know how skillful he is, but trust me when I say there are other men out there who know how to make the pussy pop too. In my opinion, Cedric is good, but I know a man who delivers nothing but greatness."

"Well, you've definitely had more sex partners than me, so I can't argue with you on that. And if whomever you're speaking of is that great, maybe you should send him my way."

Evelyn sucked her teeth, then moved her head from side to side. "No way, sweetheart. We will not share another man, and it's a damn shame that we shared Cedric. But it is what it is, and at least you know now what kind of man you were really married to."

"I do know, thanks to you." I paused to take another swig of the vodka. "But like you said, it is what it is, and the past is the past. The future is yet to be seen, but I got a feeling that I'ma need another one of those toe-curling orgasms he provides real soon. You gotta admit that the man definitely knows how to chomp down on the cooda."

Evelyn jumped from her seat to give me a high five. "Bam!" she exclaimed as she slapped her hand against mine. "I'll give him that for sure. That tongue of his be all up in there, and, girl, don't let that mutha slither near yo' ass or take a swipe at it! Boom!"

I giggled, then fell back on the sofa while kicking my feet in the air. "Yes! Yes! Yes! That tongue is fierce! I'm getting all hot and bothered just thinking about it, and I can't help but think that he's only a phone call away. Do you think I should call him?"

Evelyn moved her head like a bobblehead doll. "Yep. 'Cause he's just a phone call away. You should call him to come over tonight. Let him bend you over like this, and call you bitches and hoes while slapping yo' ass." Evelyn bent over the chair and slapped her butt. "He be smacking hard, and . . . and he'll bite that ass too."

I laughed my butt off. He'd never cursed at me, nor had he taken a bite out of my ass. But I was so sure that Cedric had *explored* many interesting things with the tricks he had cheated on me with, including Evelyn. In no way was I offended by this conversation. Cedric's dick was always on point, but after our last sex session, I never wanted him to touch me again. I was strictly talking smack because I was drunk, and I had always wanted Evelyn to discuss freely what had happened between them. I had to let her know that it didn't anger me one bit.

"Girl, you are a mess," I said, throwing my hand back at her. "I can't believe we're talking about ole Ceddy like this, but you'd better believe that if it were two men, they'd surely be talking about the woman."

"Right. And I don't know how we ventured here, because you were about to tell me something about Jacoby, weren't you?"

I scratched my head, thinking about Jacoby. It was getting late, and I hadn't heard from him. It wasn't like he often called to check in, but there were times when I worried too much about him.

"It wasn't important," I said. "But I do need to call and check on him. Where in the heck is my cell phone at?"

Evelyn stood to look around the room. She staggered a bit, then let out a loud belch. She slapped her hand over her mouth, and when her cheeks blew up like a balloon, she rushed off toward the bathroom. Unfortunately, she didn't make it. Puke sprayed on my plush carpet, and some splattered on my table. She slowly turned while holding her stomach.

"Sorry," she said in a whisper. "I'll clean it up."

"Yes, you will," I said, then shook my head as she ran the rest of the way to the bathroom.

While she was in there, I attempted to gather myself so that I could look for my phone. It was in the kitchen, and when I called Jacoby, he didn't answer. I left a message for him to call me back, and after ending the call, I dialed Cedric's number to see if he'd had any luck with reaching him. I guessed he heard the slurring of my voice.

"Yes, I talked to him, but like always, he said he would let me know. On another note, you really need to get some help. I'm concerned about you."

"Don't be. I'll be fine."

I hung up on Cedric, hoping that I would be fine, as I'd professed.

4

Evelyn

Being with my BFF's on Sunday was fun. First, we went to dinner at Outback Steakhouse, and then we went to a little hole-in-the-wall nightclub to have some drinks and to dance. Trina didn't drink as much as Kayla and me, only because one of us had to drive. Kayla was sloppy drunk, and we had to hold her up as we carried her through the door of her condo. When we entered, we found Jacoby and his girlfriend in the living room area, watching TV. They looked like they were up to no good, causing Kayla to straighten her back and wave her hands around.

"Up, up. Hands in the air," she ordered, slurring. "I need to make sure y'all are not over there doing any of that freaky stuff."

Jacoby's girlfriend laughed, but he sat there with an embarrassed look on his face. Kayla blew him a kiss before we carried her off to her bedroom and laid her back on the bed.

"Stop making such a big fuss over me," she said, trying to push us away. "I'm fine. Get out and go home so I can get some sleep."

Sleep was exactly what she needed. Trina pulled back the sheets, and after tucking Kayla in bed and turning off the lights, we left her bedroom. As I closed the door behind us, I listened to Kayla sing Mary J.'s "No More Drama," which played on the intercom.

"She's a mess," Trina said, turning to me. "Y'all had too much to drink, and I'm surprised you're still standing."

"I'm good. I knew when to stop, even though my head is banging."

As we made our way toward the front door, we stopped to say good-bye to Jacoby and his girlfriend. She was kind of on the thick side. I was surprised to see Jacoby with a chick who had so much weave too. As tall and as handsome as he was, I expected better from him.

"We'll lock the door on our way out," Trina said. "Check on your mother in a few hours and call me if she doesn't seem okay."

"She'll be fine. She's like that all the time. By morning, she won't remember a thing."

Trina and I looked at each other. It appeared that Kayla was starting to have a serious problem with alcohol. Cedric had mentioned it to me, but I hadn't taken his claim seriously. But after witnessing her toss back all that alcohol tonight, I knew she had a problem.

We stood at the door, about to leave, but I stopped and asked Jacoby if he would get me a few aspirin. I didn't have any at home, and I didn't want Trina to have to stop and get me some. As I waited for Jacoby, Trina told me to meet her in the car. Seconds later, he came out of the bathroom and handed the aspirin to me.

"Thanks," I said.

He didn't reply. I could sense that he was still bitter about my actions from the past. He knew all about my affair with Cedric. And I was sure thoughts of my inappropriate advances toward him were fresh in his head. As he looked down at the floor to avoid eye contact with me, I reached out and lifted his chin.

"I know this may seem a little awkward for you, but just so you know, I'm sorry for everything that I did. I never meant to hurt you, but I was stupid, and I did some crazy things just to get money. That's all in the past, okay? And just as Trina said to you before leaving, if you ever need anything, let us know. We're like family. A little dysfunctional at times, but we love each other, nonetheless."

Jacoby nodded. "Thanks for saying that. Take care, and I'll tell my moms to call you in the morning and let you know she's okay."

"Is she really okay? I'm a little worried about her. Should I be?"

He shrugged, then took a hard swallow. "You'll have to ask her. I don't know what's going on in her head."

I didn't think that I could get Jacoby to speak up about what was really going on, so I left it there. I walked to the car, thinking about my interesting night with my BFF's. It had been a long time since we'd kicked it like we did tonight. It had felt good to get turned up. Trina and I laughed about it in the car, but our conversation quickly got serious when we talked about Kayla.

"When is the last time you saw her sober?" I asked. "She's been working that bottle, and she really did consume a lot of alcohol tonight."

"Yeah, but so did you. I think tonight was long overdue. Kayla was out to have a good time. She stays cooped up in that condo a lot. Her whole life revolves around Jacoby, and I think it felt good for her to get out tonight. We need to do that more often."

"I agree. And I do understand what you're saying about Kayla, but let's keep our eyes on her. It seems as if she may be going through something, and I don't think it has anything to do with Cedric."

Trina tapped her fingers on the steering wheel while driving. "If not, what do you think it is?"

"I don't know. I was hoping that you'd be able to tell me."

"I can't tell you what I don't know. Out of all of us, Kayla has always been the private one. I hope everything is okay, and if there is something severely wrong, I'm sure she'll eventually tell us."

We continued to talk about Kayla, but then our conversation switched to her and Keith. I had a few questions about his father, but I didn't quite know how to get the information I wanted without seeming too nosy or as if I was up to something.

"I just wish Keith would lighten up and look at things from a different perspective," Trina said. "He's so narrow minded, and it drives me crazy sometimes."

"That's how most men are, so don't trip too hard. Keith loves you and you love him. The two of you will be able to work through whatever."

"I truly hope so. Lord knows, I hope so, 'cause I do not want to lose him."

Trina was always talking in circles. I could tell she wanted to tell me something, and if not today, she would spill her guts to me at a later date. She wasn't as private as Kayla was.

"Why do you think you may lose him? Something must be going on, but if you don't want to share, I'm good with that. I already know how you feel about me knowing your business."

Trina stopped at a red light, then glanced at herself in the rearview mirror. She moved her short bangs away from her forehead, then wiped her finger across her dry lips.

"There's nothing going on with us. There's more going on with *me*. While we were in New York, we hung out with this chick named Sasha. I've been chatting with her over the phone about some of my paintings, and she insists that she can put some money in my pockets and help me make a real name for myself in the industry."

"And? What's so wrong with that?"

Trina shrugged. "Nothing, I guess. Except that I'm starting to think about her maybe more than I should be."

When the light turned green, she drove off. She didn't dare turn her head to look at me. I totally didn't get my BFF's. They both had it all, but they always managed to fuck things up. As far as I could see, Keith was the best man that any woman could hope for. He was fine as fuck, sexy as hell, and God fearing, and he had money. He had his own crib, owned three cars, and had a career. But there Trina was, talking to me about catching feelings for a bitch in New York that she barely knew. I wasn't sure how to respond. The last thing I wanted to do was come off as being too judgmental and harsh.

"You can think about whomever you wish," I said. "But I hope you're not planning on pursuing this chick. Keith would be devastated, and after what happened to him because of that other crazy broad you was dating, Lexi, you may want to rethink those feelings you're having."

She had the audacity to catch an attitude with me. Her head snapped to the side, and she tried to pull back on what she'd said.

"It wasn't like I just told you I was falling in love with someone else. I know that Keith would be devastated, and I will never forget what Lexi did to him. All I said was I'd been thinking about her. A thought never hurt anyone. I have no intentions to pursue a relationship with her, and all I'm doing right now is rambling."

"Are you sure about not trying to pursue a relationship with her? If you're going to allow her to, as you put it, help you with your career, how do you know what that will lead to?"

"It will lead to nothing. Nothing at all, because I love Keith, and that's all there is to it."

I wasn't convinced. And people always saw me as the bad person. Hell, yeah, I was, but I wasn't about to give Trina a pass on this one. She wanted a bitch like me to come along and steal her man. And while I failed at trying to get him on my team, that didn't mean another woman would fail. I left well enough alone and tried to change the subject. I was sure she would appreciate me doing so.

"How long have Keith's parents been married?" I questioned.

She shrugged. "I'm not sure. Maybe twenty or thirty years. All I know is for a long time. I think they were high school sweethearts. Why?"

"I was just asking. I had no idea you were dating a man with wealthy parents like that. That's great, and I often think about what people do to make that kind of money. What kind of work does his father do, or was the money inherited?"

"Some of it was inherited, but very little. I think a lot of his dad's money comes from investments and business deals that he's made over the years. He also works for the government, but I can't really say what he does. All I know is that whatever it is, it's legal."

"I would hope so. I mean, does he have an office or anything like that? Or does he work from that beautiful house they live in? And speaking of that house, why haven't you said anything to me about it? It is off the chain, and talk about somebody who was shocked."

"I know. I was stunned when I first saw it too. Keith kind of kept it a secret from me. I guess he didn't want me to know how much money they were sitting on. His father's office, though, is in Chesterfield, right across from the mall. It's a tall white building with mirrorlike windows on it. Keith and I stopped by there a few times to drop him off some things. Like I said, I don't know exactly what he does, but that office he sits in is sick too."

I didn't want Trina to get too suspicious, so I left it right there. I had been thinking about paying Charles a visit. Now that I knew where he worked, maybe I would follow through with my plan. For now, though, Charles had to wait. I had to deal with Cedric, who showed up at my apartment ten minutes after Trina dropped me off. He never called to say he was coming over, and we had to be careful, because I didn't want Trina or Kayla to know he and I were involved.

I hurried to let him inside, then quickly shut the door.

"What is it, Cedric? It's late, and I need to get some beauty rest."

"I stopped by to see if you've made any progress with Kayla. Has she told you anything? You stopped by to see her the other day. Y'all had dinner, then went out to kick it. I'm sure she told you something."

"She was too drunk to say anything. I will say that she mentioned something about you and Jacoby, but she didn't elaborate on it."

He didn't like my response. His face twisted and he winced. "What in the hell is that supposed to mean . . . ? She mentioned something? What did she mention?"

I folded my arms and caught a quick attitude with him too. "First of all, lower your voice. What I meant was, she said that something about you and Jacoby was bothering her. That could have been anything. I tried to get her to say more, but she was so drunk that she changed the subject and started talking about you and her having sex with each other recently. I had no idea you were still fucking her."

I was sure he didn't want to have this conversation, and even if he was or wasn't, I didn't care. In the past, it had bothered me. I had wanted it over between the two of them, and I had done my best to make sure Cedric kept his sex life with her down to a minimum. Today it was a different ball game for sure.

Cedric waved me off, then went into my bedroom. My thoughts about him not wanting to hear this were confirmed. I followed behind him, only to listen to more of his bullshit.

"Who I fuck is no one's business," he said, wiggling his tie away from his neck. "The bottom line is, we had a deal. You got what the fuck you wanted, and I'm still waiting to get what I wanted. What in the hell is taking you so long to find out what she and Jacoby are up to?"

"I told you this will take some time. Kayla doesn't completely trust me yet. I'm working hard at getting her back on my team. You never gave me a specific time frame to get this information to you, so you just have to wait, unless you want to do some type of investigation of your own."

He sat on the bed and started to remove his leather shoes. "Investigation, my ass. I took care of you, and now it's time for you to take care of me. You got two more weeks, Evelyn. Two more weeks or else."

"Or else what?"

He snatched my arm, then pulled me to him. As I attempted to pull away, he pushed me back on the bed, then lay on top of me. "I can show you better than I can tell you. Just keep that two-week time frame in your head while you open your goddamned legs."

Cedric attempted to pry my legs open with his, but I resisted. He stopped, then gave me a hard kiss on the mouth. While kissing me, he flipped up my skirt and slipped a few finger underneath my panties. Several of his fingers entered my pussy. A high arch formed in my back, and I squirmed around as he worked his thick fingers in and out of me.

"How was dinner tonight?" he asked while fingering me.

I answered with my eyes shut tight, trying to pretend that I was enjoying this, just so this night wouldn't turn ugly. "Good, but never better than this."

"Well, I have something even better. Keep your eyes shut and enjoy."

He lowered himself and took oral sex to new heights when he fucked me with his tongue. I couldn't deny that Kayla was so right. He was pretty good at this.

The next day, I put the thoughts of what had happened between Cedric and me behind me. I was excited about going to pay Charles a visit. I had a burgundy, V-neck, fitted dress on that showed a healthy portion of my cleavage. A thin black belt was secured around my waist, and I had topped it all off with red-bottom shoes. My straightened hair fell past my shoulders and was parted down the middle.

As I strutted into his office building, I worked my curvy hips from side to side, causing both men and women to turn their heads in my direction. I wasn't sure if Charles would take time from his busy schedule to see me, but the second I got off the elevator, I spotted him conversing with two men, who were standing close to him. When they turned their heads, so did he. The expression on his face turned flat. He squinted to make sure I was the same woman who had come to his house. I confirmed who I was when I walked up to him and asked if we could go somewhere private to talk.

"Sure," he said, then excused himself from the other conversation.

As we walked past the receptionist's desk, he stopped to address her. "Hold my calls for about fifteen or twenty minutes. I'm going into a meeting."

"Yes, sir," the receptionist said. "Will do."

He motioned for me to follow him, and I had no problem doing so. I checked him out as we went. He was wearing black leather shoes and black slacks with suspenders that looked like they were straight off the rack at Armani. His well-pressed burgundy shirt showcased his muscles, and his coal-black waves, which showed a hint of gray, had sharp lines. I had no words for his trimmed goatee, and I loved men with rich black skin. His whole persona turned me on. Today he looked more like Keith, without all the muscles and tattoos, than like Bryson. I knew that I had to have my shit together when confronting Charles, and knowing that time wasn't on my side, I decided it was in my best interests to get straight to the point.

"Have a seat," he said as we stepped into his spacious office. To the right of his mahogany desk sat a sofa and two chairs. A glass table stood in the middle of the seating arrangement, and on top of it was an array of business magazines. Many plaques covered his walls, and pictures of him and his wife, as well as their family, were propped up here and there. His entire office was surrounded by windows that afforded a view of Highway 40 and part of the city of Chesterfield.

We both sat on the sofa, but before he actually took a seat, he asked if I wanted a beverage. "I can ask my secretary to get whatever you'd like," he said politely.

His secretary couldn't give me what I wanted. Only he could. But instead of saying that, I crossed my legs, then cleared my throat. "No, thank you. I already had lunch, and the cranberry juice I had with it was fine."

"Okay. Now, tell me why you're here. I hope your visit doesn't have anything else to do with Bryson, and I also hope that it has nothing to do with you asking for more money. My wife and I aren't prepared to give you more than we've already given you. The agreement was very clear. You did understand it, didn't you?"

"Of course I did. And I wouldn't dare come here to ask you for any more money. You've already given me enough. I'm very appreciative of your generous gift. It has changed my life in many ways."

Seeming relieved, he released a deep sigh. He rubbed his hands together and then wiped one across his forehead.

"I also didn't come here to discuss Bryson," I continued. "I haven't heard one word from him, and I'm very pleased about that."

"Let's just say that he's on an extended vacation. You won't be hearing from him anytime soon. His mother and I have made sure of that."

That pleased me. I hoped he was somewhere burning in hell. But after speaking to his mother, I was sure that Bryson was somewhere on an island, relaxing and stirring up more trouble.

"The reason that I'm here goes a little something like this," I said. "I honestly cannot stop thinking about you. From the second I laid my eyes on you, I have felt something strange. Something I've never felt before, and I refuse to ignore what I'm feeling inside. I had to come here and share this with you. I'm a very confident woman, and I was always taught to pursue my dreams. Like the one I had about us the other night. I would love to tell you all about it, but only if you want to hear how things went down."

Charles remained silent as he sat next to me. I had a difficult time reading him. There was no expression on his face whatsoever, and he damn near looked like he wasn't even breathing. He was still. Calm. Cool and very collected. I figured he was pondering what to say, and while he was in deep thought, I continued.

"I don't know how things are with you and your wife, and quite frankly, I don't care. All I would like to do is spend one day with you. Just one, and if you demand more time with me, you're more than welcome to it. If not, so be it. I'll move on and pretend that this conversation between us never took place."

Charles still hadn't said anything. He did, however, get up and strut over to his desk. He opened a drawer, then pulled out something that looked like a plaque. He observed the plaque while sitting on the edge of his desk.

"I just got this the other day," he said, still looking at it. "The inscription reads, 'Charles Vincent Washington, MVP.' This is, like, my tenth award, and as you look around my office, you can see for yourself that I'm quite a successful man. I am saying that to you because I need a few minutes to gather myself before responding to what you just said. I'm searching for the right words, just so I don't, you know, hurt your feelings.

"While I think you're one sexy-ass woman, I have to ask if you are out of your goddamned mind. I didn't get this far in life by fucking around with tricks like you. I've always had a very supportive woman by my side, one whom I love and one whom I would never betray. My family means everything to me, and I've raised my sons to be outstanding men who make smart decisions and who don't need side hoes like you to make them feel good. That's why I'm highly disappointed with Bryson, and you—"

He had gone too far, so I quickly stood to cut him off. "That's right. Speak for one of your sons and not the other. One may very well be a man, but the other one comes off as a spoiled rotten bitch with no morals or values. I didn't come here to hurt *your* feelings, but insulting me was the wrong thing to do. I am way more than a side ho or a trick, and if you had taken the opportunity to get to know me better, you would know that. But thanks for letting me know how much you love your wife and how would never betray her. That's a beautiful thing. I applaud your dedication to her, and kudos to you and all your success. Keep up the good work, Charles. I'm sure I'll see you again, and maybe next time you'll be singing a new tune."

"There won't be a next time. Get the hell out of my office, and don't ever come back here again."

His nastiness was totally uncalled for. No wonder Bryson acted a fool as he did. He had got it all from ole dad. That was how I knew Charles wasn't the so-called loving husband he claimed to be.

With my feelings slightly bruised, I walked out of his office and headed to my car. I was less than two blocks away when I heard my phone vibrating inside my purse. I reached for it, then looked to see who it was. The caller came across as unknown, but I answered, anyway.

"Hello," I said with a sharp tone.

"Evelyn," the woman said. "If you thought my son beat your ass, I assure you that what I will do to you is a whole lot worse. Stay away from my damn husband or else."

I laughed at him for telling her about my visit, and at her for being so insecure as to call me. Without replying, I hung up on her. What she was unware of was the fact that I loved a challenge. And had she not called, I might have left well enough alone. It was time to carry on, and I was now in hot pursuit of Charles.

5

Trina

I was wrong, and I knew it this time. For the past two nights, while Keith was asleep, I had been on the phone with Sasha. At first, our conversations had been all about business. But then things had taken a turn when she told me about her girlfriend and her having problems. Tonight I shot her some encouraging words, and before I knew it, we began to click. She thanked me for listening to her, and she said she wished that I was there to help take away some of her pain.

"Whether I'm there or not," I whispered to her, "please keep your head up. I get how frustrating relationships can be, and nobody's relationship is perfect."

She sniffled, then said, "Not even your and Keith's? The two of you seem so happy together. I watched the two of you while you were here. I could sense the love. I can only wish for a relationship like that, but it's been real hectic around here. Diamond is never home anymore. When she is here, all we do is argue. She speaks real ill to me, and I think she's cheating on me with a man."

I thought I heard someone on the steps, but when I got up to see if someone was there, I didn't see anyone. I returned to the sofa and tucked my legs underneath me, sitting on them.

"If it's that bad, Sasha, then end it. Life is too short to be unhappy. I never would have thought that a woman as beautiful as you are would be in a relationship like that. You came across as having it all together. If your woman is preventing you from being all that you can be, then you know what you have to do."

"You're right. And again, thanks for listening to me. It's been one of those days, but I'll get through this. In the meantime, you really should come to New York. We can have ourselves a lot of fun, and I want to introduce you to some people who can really help you. I showed them some of the paintings you did while you were here. They were floored."

I couldn't help but smile. "I haven't decided when I'll be coming back that way, but it may be soon. I'll let you know for sure. Meanwhile, keep your head up and do you."

"Okay, my sista. Stay pretty and we'll talk soon."

"You too."

After we ended the call, I sat on the sofa, in deep thought. I needed to take that trip to New York just to see if Sasha and her friends would really be able to help me like she claimed they would. It would be foolish of me not to go and see what was up—too foolish—even though Keith wouldn't approve.

I went into the kitchen to get some water. While guzzling it down, I glanced at the clock on the wall, which showed that it was almost one o'clock in the morning. I hadn't realized that I'd been talking to Sasha for that long, and I was sure that by now Keith was in a deep sleep. I climbed the stairs in my sweatpants and tank top, which was cut above my midriff. Keith and I had gone and worked out earlier, and I still hadn't taken a shower. My muscles were a little sore, so instead of jumping into the bed with him, I tiptoed by the bed and made my way to the bathroom.

Before entering the bathroom, I stood near the doorway and looked at him in bed as he snored. A thin white sheet covered his bottom half, and I could see a sizable hump where the good stuff was. His colorful tattoos showed on his arms and chest, and I had a serious desire to kiss those thick lips. I hurriedly showered, and dripping wet and without any clothes on, I quietly climbed on top of him. As I massaged his chest, his eyes began to open. A slight smile appeared on his face as his eyes scanned my body, and his hands began to roam my curves. He traced my hourglass figure, then sucked in a deep breath.

"Sexy, sexy, sexy," he said while now massaging my breasts.

I could feel his dick rising to the occasion, and I was eager to remove the sheet that stood in our way. I pulled it away from him, then comfortably straddled his lap again. He flexed his neck from side to side and closed his eyes as he started to tickle my pearl. Within seconds, my juices started to flow, causing me to put a slow grind in motion.

"Your pussy is so sweet, juicy looking, and perfect for me. And did you know that I love to watch your fluids drip and ooze right into the crack of your ass? That's why I can't keep my mouth off of it."

I laughed, then lean forward to finally kiss his thick lips. "Yeah, well, then maybe you should take action and do something about those juices. Better off in your mouth than on the sheets."

"I concur. So I suggest that you lie on your stomach and let me enter as I please."

"Of course."

I removed myself from his lap, then lay on my stomach. Keith lay beside me, with one of his legs crossed over mine. His cold fingertips ran up and down my spine and through the crack of my ass, giving my whole body a tickle.

"That feels sooo good," I said, with my head on the pillow and my eyes closed. "There is something about your touch that sets me on fire."

Keith was a gentle lovemaker. On very few occasions was he rough with me, and that was normally when he was upset with me or mad about something else. His soft lips touched my shoulders, then my back. From my back, they traveled to my ass. That was when he moved from beside me and kneeled between my legs. He then buried his face in my ass and sucked my juices that flowed near my anal hole. I hiked my butt up high just so he could have as much access as he needed. From one hole to the other, he set my entire body on fire. I shivered all over and cried out his name when he turned on his back and carefully placed my pussy lips over his mouth. His tongue traveled deeper. He brought it out to toy with my belly ring, and then he locked my pussy in place and tore it up. I was out of breath as I ground on top of him. My legs quickly got weak, and my curled toes were squeezed tight.

"I lovvve you," I cried out. "Damn, I love you, and I don't ever want you to stop loving meee."

He couldn't respond, as he had a mouthful, but it wasn't long before he fired back at me. By then his dick was as far in me as it could go. I was on my back, with my legs poured over his broad shoulders.

"I love you too," he said while looking down at me with so much passion in his eyes. "And I will never stop loving you."

I was so emotional. Tears seeped from the corners of my eyes as we rocked our sexy bodies together. Keith and I were perfect for each other. I couldn't ask for more, and I made a silent vow in that moment never to converse with Sasha again.

***

The bright sun rays came through the window, letting me know that morning had arrived. With a slight headache, I turned in bed, only to see that Keith was gone. On the nightstand was a beautiful red rose, along with a note. I reached out to see what it said. It read: *Had some errands to run this morning. Didn't want to interrupt your beauty sleep. See you around noon. Love you.*

I smiled, then pulled the sheets back to get out of bed. My whole body was sore from the workout we'd gotten in last night. I needed a long, hot shower, so I staggered into the bathroom to handle my business. I must've stayed in there for about thirty minutes, and when I turned off the cold water, I heard my cell phone ringing. I wrapped my body with a towel, then walked over to the nightstand to answer my phone. It had stopped ringing, but I could see that I had seven missed calls. They all were from Kayla's phone. I hurried to call her back, praying that everything was okay. When Jacoby answered, I held my breath.

"Can you come over here, please?" he said, with frustration in his voice. "My mother is passed out on the kitchen floor. I've been trying to get her up, but she keeps going in and out. I've never seen her like this, and I'm starting to get worried."

"Does she need an ambulance? I'm on my way, but maybe you need to call an ambulance."

"She's drunk as shit," he said. "I don't think she needs an ambulance. She needs to talk to someone who can help her. I tried talking to her, but she won't listen to me."

"Okay. I'm on my way. Thanks for calling me."

I rushed to put on some clothes, then made my way to Kayla's place. On the way there, I called Evelyn to see if she could meet me.

"What's going on with her?" she asked.

"I don't know. But she's putting a lot of stress on Jacoby. I can sense it in his voice. I think it's time for us to step in."

"I was on my way to the nail shop, but I'll meet you there within the hour."

"Thanks. See you soon."

Right after I ended my call with her, my phone rang again. I thought it was Jacoby calling me back, but instead, it was Sasha. I didn't bother to answer. Eventually, I would tell her that I wasn't interested in her help, and that I wouldn't be coming to New York. I just didn't need anything or anyone to interfere with my relationship with Keith. Even though I could surely use some additional money, a visit to New York just didn't make sense right now.

Financially, I had to do something, though. I hadn't been to the studio to get any work done in about three months. Keith was holding down most of the bills, and we both understood that if we didn't sell our artwork, we basically didn't have money. It had been a long time since I'd had any interior-decorating gigs too. I thought about putting out an ad to spread the word about my services.

When I got to Kayla's condo, I saw Evelyn's car parked in the lot. She must've rushed to get here. When I got inside, I saw that she and Jacoby had put Kayla on the sofa. They were trying to get her to snap out of it by shaking her. Her arms flopped around, and she kept slurring a bunch of nonsense about the sky not being blue.

"It's actually purple, if you look hard enough, and no . . . no one can deny that it's a *beautiful* day in the neighborhood, isn't it?" she said, smiling at me.

Her eyes were bugged out, and if I didn't know any better, I would have thought that Kayla was on drugs. The flimsy dress she wore hung off her shoulders, and we could all tell that she had lost a lot of weight. She squinted, then threw her hand back at me.

"Trina, girl, is that you? I almost couldn't tell with that ugly ole frown on your face."

She laughed, but my frown deepened. I hated to see my best friend like this. It tore me to pieces, and I would do whatever I could to help her get back on track. But first, she needed to come clean and tell us what was really going on with her.

We all helped her off the sofa and escorted her to the bedroom. Evelyn headed toward the bathroom to run her some bathwater, but I told her that I didn't think a bath was a good idea.

"She's too weak. Maybe a shower would be better. She can sit on the seat and wash herself."

Jacoby went to get us some towels, as well as some clean clothes that she could change into. I hated for him to see his mother like this, so when he returned to the bedroom, I suggested that he leave the house.

"We can handle her from here," I said. "Go hang out with your friends or something. I'll call to let you know if we need anything else."

"Are you sure?" he said, looking at his watch. "I'm supposed to be at band camp right now. But I didn't want to leave her like this."

"She'll be fine. All she needs is a shower and some rest. Maybe a little counseling too."

"I agree. I'm leaving, but don't forget to call me if you guys need anything."

Jacoby left. Evelyn and I lifted Kayla from the bed—she had fallen asleep that fast. We carried her into the bathroom, and after sitting her on the seat in the shower, with her clothes on, Evelyn turned on the cold water. The water sprayed all over Kayla, causing her to snap out of it and cover her face with her hands.

"Wha . . . what are y'all doing? Turn that cold water off!" she shouted, then stuck out her hand to touch the faucet. She couldn't reach it. I turned the water to warm so she would sit still.

"Relax," I said. "When you feel that you can stand, take your clothes off and wash yourself. Evelyn and I will be in your bedroom, waiting for you, when you come out."

"Waiting on me?" she spat. "Ugh! That's nasty. I don't do women, and you already know that I'm only interested in men. There is no reason for y'all to be waiting for me in the bedroom."

I ignored her comment. After all, she didn't know what she was saying. We left the bathroom, but from a short distance, we could see Kayla struggling to take off her clothes. She kept cussing and fussing about something. And when she finally got her clothes off, she fell back on the seat and started to cry. Seeing her cry brought tears to my eyes. I looked at Evelyn, whose eyes were filled with tears too, but she hurried to blink them away.

"Do we allow her to get it all out or go in there with her?" Evelyn said. "I feel horrible for her. She really needs to get some help."

I agreed, then went into the bathroom with Kayla. Evelyn followed me. I kneeled beside the shower door, while Evelyn stood close behind me.

"What is it?" I asked Kayla. "Why are you doing this to yourself? If you're going through something, please tell us and stop trying to act as if everything is okay. We're your friends. We're only here to help."

Still seated, Kayla wiped her flowing tears, and then she wiped snot from her nose. She squeezed her eyes together, then lightly banged the back of her head against the glass.

"Please leave," she said. "I don't want nobody to see me like this. I want to be alone."

"We're not going to leave you like this," Evelyn said. "Take your shower, and when you're done, we're going to be right here waiting for you."

"Right," I added. "Say what you want and get mad if you wish. We're not going anywhere."

Kayla didn't even look our way. She just sat there, releasing her emotions. We went back into her bedroom, and as I kept my eyes on her, I could see her starting to wash up. Within an hour, she came out of the bathroom with a pink robe covering her. The first thing she did was walk over to a small cabinet that had liquor inside of it.

"Where's Jacoby?" she said in a soft tone. She lifted an almost empty bottle of Hennessy, then twirled it around.

"Please put that down." I stood to go remove the bottle from her hand. She snatched it away as I reached for it, and held on tight to it.

"Don't come into my home, trying to tell me what to do. If I want to have a little drink, I will do it."

"She's not trying to tell you what to do," Evelyn said from her perch on the bed. "She's just trying to prevent you from making a big mistake."

Kayla snapped her head to the side and gave Evelyn a look that could kill. She narrowed her eyes, then gritted her teeth. "Don't you dare talk to me about mistakes, especially when you've made plenty of them, missy."

Evelyn hopped up from the bed, then snatched up her purse. "I figured all of this had something to do with your feelings about me. And there is no need for you to pretend that you've forgiven me, when you haven't. If being around me is causing you this much pain, then I'll leave and never come back here again. I know what I did was wrong, but damn. How many times am I going to have to apologize? How many times will I be attacked for doing what I did with Cedric?" Evelyn's voice started to crack. "I'm tired of this crap, and forgive me for thinking that we had left what had happened in the past." Now Evelyn was crying.

I wasn't as emotional as the two of them were, and like always, I was caught in the middle. "Calm down, Evelyn. We came here to see about Kayla and find out what, exactly, is troubling her. I'm sure you want to know too, so let's not make this all about you."

"All about *me*?" Evelyn said, pointing to her chest. "It's never been about *me*, Trina. Ever since the day I was born, it hasn't been about me. As I sit here watching Kayla, all I can think about is my drunk-ass mother. How she ignored me and gave all her attention to my father. How all I was to him was a punching bag and a sex toy. I'm not trying to make anything all about me, and I'm not going to stand here and take the blame for everybody's damn problems. My mother blamed me for hers, you blamed me for yours, and now Kayla is standing there, once again blaming me for hers. This is just . . . just too much."

Evelyn charged toward the door, but Kayla reached out to stop her. She grabbed her arm real tight but spoke with a calm voice. "I'm not blaming you as much as I blame myself. You will never understand what it feels like to lose everything that you had and have to start all over. While I'm glad that my divorce from Cedric is final, this shit still hurts. We spent many years together, and it's hard on me to wake up every morning alone. It feels funny doing everything by myself, and I hate that Jacoby doesn't have a father figure around."

Kayla went on. "Some days are good, but other days are bad. And like Trina said, this has very little to do with you. Yes, I'm still a little bitter about what you did, but I also know that Cedric used you. He saw a broken woman with an unfortunate past, and he took advantage of your vulnerabilities. It had nothing to do with his love for you, and I know that now."

"Then why do I feel as if you still hate me?" Evelyn said tearfully. "I know you, Kayla, and things are not the same as they used to be. The way you look at me says it all. Given how you speak to me, I can tell you're still angry. I don't want to be here if you don't want me here. But the truth is, I love you and Trina. I just don't know how to show the two of you how sorry I am for everything that I did."

"The first thing you can do is stop apologizing," I said. "We hear you loud and clear. It's just that we got our own problems too. And when we tend to think about all our problems, we may focus too much on where those problems originated from. Kayla can't think about her failed marriage without putting you into the equation. You played a big part in that, even though Cedric had been messing around with numerous other women, as well. What Kayla has to do is come to grips with it being over. She needs to celebrate her departure from him and realize that it really is a good thing. That may take some time, but during the process, it will take time for her to have that trusting and loving friendship with you again."

"I couldn't have said it better," Kayla said with a nod. "Just give me more time. I'm almost there, and the truth is, I'm on a downward spiral because of something that is bothering me about Jacoby and Cedric. If I tell the two of you about it, y'all probably won't believe me. I'm so worried about my son, and I don't know what Cedric will do if he ever finds out the real deal behind him being shot."

Kayla sat down on the bed, in tears, and then told us about Jacoby's plot to have Cedric killed. He was the one who had gone to Paula Daniels and had asked her to do the dirty work. She was paid a substantial amount of money, but when Jacoby went back to her to call off the deal, Paula moved forward. She wanted Cedric dead, and there was no changing her mind. Kayla had no idea why Paula hadn't said anything about it to anyone yet, but she knew that Paula had been trying to get Cedric to come see her in jail. Kayla truly felt that if he found out the truth, Cedric would contact the police and have Jacoby arrested. And to her, that could happen any day.

"I'm just so worried," Kayla said, barely able to catch her breath as she cried. "I want to tell Cedric, but I can't go behind my baby's back and do that. What if he goes to jail? He would never make it in there, and I do not want to lose my only child."

Evelyn and I sat down on the bed and embraced Kayla. "You're not going to lose him," Evelyn said. "We'll think of something, and we need to do it fast, especially if Paula is trying to reach out to Cedric."

"I agree," Kayla said. "It's just a matter of time before Cedric changes his mind about going to see her. I know that she's been writing him, but he never opens her letters to read them. What if he decides to open them? What if she writes to him and tells him exactly how things went down?"

"I guess I must have too much faith in Cedric," I said. "I don't believe that he would contact the police and have Jacoby arrested. After all, he does consider Jacoby his son. He loves him, and would never do anything like that to destroy him."

Kayla and Evelyn snapped their heads to the side and looked at me as if I were crazy.

"You don't know Cedric," they said in unison.

"He would put his mama behind bars if he thought she'd betrayed him," Kayla said. "I'm well aware of the man I was married to, and ever since he got shot, Cedric has been a changed man. I can see it in his eyes. In my heart, I truly believe that he's up to something."

We all sat silent for a while. I then tried to convince them that Cedric wouldn't harm Jacoby, but then I got to the point where I was trying to convince myself. This was one big mess. Now I understood why Kayla had been doing so much drinking. We discussed her new habit, and she said that it was under control. I didn't believe her, and Evelyn and I promised to check on her every single day.

6

Kayla

I felt a little better. Trina and Evelyn left a few hours later, and right after they left, I called Jacoby to find out where he was. The two of us needed to talk, and the first thing I needed to do was apologize to him for the way I'd been acting. I knew that seeing me drunk all the time was affecting him. I just couldn't stop causing my son harm, and that made me feel horrible. I told him that as I spoke to him over the phone, and I asked him to come home soon.

"I don't like to see you that way, but stop worrying so much about me," he said. "And if you don't mind, I won't be home until later. Some of the fellas and me are going to hang out at the mall. After that, Adrianne's mom wants me to help her paint their kitchen. I told her that I would."

"Okay. Have a good time, and please know that I can't help worrying about you. You definitely know why. Have you spoken to Cedric again?"

"I have. I told him I'll try to catch up with him next weekend. Maybe I do need to start doing some things with him again. That way he'll get off my back."

"That may bc a good idca. It makes him suspicious when you distance yourself. He continues to ask me what is wrong with you, and it makes me feel awkward when I have to keep telling him that I don't know."

"Well, whatever you do, don't tell him anything. I'm thinking that maybe I should say something to him myself. If he hears it from me, maybe he'll understand."

"No. He would never understand, and I would never want you in a situation where you're alone with him, talking about what you did. I don't trust Cedric. He's a vicious man when he wants to be, and you already know that."

Jacoby said that he wouldn't say anything to Cedric, but he also could have said that just to get off the phone and get back to his friends. His social life was much better than mine was. I couldn't believe how much I had been cooped up inside since my divorce. I had had so much fun with Evelyn and Trina the other night. I needed to get out more, so I decided to put on some clothes and go have a few drinks. Many of the bars downtown were open because of the baseball game. It was the perfect time to meet people and watch the game somewhere near Ballpark Village. I'd thought about asking Trina if she wanted to go, but she had already taken enough time away from her day to see about me.

So within the hour, I was dressed in my Cardinals' T-shirt and skinny jeans. My hair had a shine to it, and with a little makeup on, I felt good. It was almost time for me to have my long lashes redone, but tonight they worked for me. I climbed in my car and headed in the direction of Ballpark Village. I spotted a bar and grill less than two blocks from the stadium and Ballpark Village. From the street, the small joint looked very crowded, as people sat outside at tables that had umbrellas. I parked and went in.

On the inside, the place was packed. Several big-screen TVs were on the walls, and the place was so noisy that I could barely hear the game. Many people sat at tables, and some were at the bar. I saw a few empty chairs at the end of the bar, so I made my way to it and sat right in front of four African American women who looked to be having a good time. They spoke to me as I took a seat and waited for the bartender. I spoke back, but my attention was focused on the bartender, who was spending way too much time waiting on someone else. I was eager to get a drink.

Almost ten minutes later, he came over to my side of the bar. He laid a napkin in front of me, then asked what I wanted to drink.

"Vodka and cranberry juice, no ice. A double shot, if you don't mind."

As the bartender made my drink, my eyes scanned the crowded place. There was a diverse group of people there, but the majority were white. I spotted a few brothas sitting in the far corner, by the restroom, and another group sat by a jukebox. Most people, however, were tuned in to the game, and plenty of drinks, wings, and burgers were being served.

"Here you are," the bartender said. "Your drink has already been taken care of by the gentleman over there."

The waiter pointed to a white man who was standing at the other end of the bar. He lifted his glass, then nodded with a smile. I didn't hesitate to smile back. After all, he was very handsome. A little young for my taste, but he had the looks of Adam Levine written all over him. His jet-black hair was spiked on top, and his beautiful light brown eyes hooked me right away. I blushed as he continued to look at me, and within a matter of minutes, there he was, standing right before me.

"Tell me," he said, "what modeling agency do you work for?"

"Oh, I wish I could tell you. There was a time when I wanted to be a model, but then life happened, and those dreams went right out the window."

"I'm sorry to hear that. But you are stunning. I hope you don't mind me buying you a drink. It's the least I can do for such a beautiful woman."

Yes, he was putting it on pretty darn thick, but I didn't care. I loved every bit of it. It was so refreshing to sit next to a man who filled my head with compliments and who had on some smell-good cologne. The black V-neck T-shirt he rocked melted on his muscles, and I could see how cut his abs were through his shirt. He was rather thin, though, but his jeans seemed to fit him in all the right places.

"I don't mind you buying me a drink, but the next one is on me. Thank you, and I do appreciate your compliments."

"Then I'll keep them coming. But before I do, my name is Justin. Justin McIntosh."

"I'm Kayla. I don't give out my last name unless I really know a person. That has always been one of my rules."

He pulled back the chair next to me, then took a seat. "I get that. Truly I do, but I'm hoping that when all is said and done, you'll get to know me much better. And if you have any more rules, I certainly want to know all about them."

We both laughed, and for the next hour or so, we indulged in an interesting conversation that revealed much more about him. He was only twenty-nine years old, he lived in an apartment complex that was less than fifteen minutes away from where I lived, and he had a degree in computer science. He had a four-year-old daughter, and he'd never been married. I gave him the scoop on me, and I told him that I had recently divorced.

"You don't have to go into the details about why that happened, but he had to be a fool to lose a woman as sexy as you."

"Well, being sexy doesn't keep a man at home and faithful these days. Not that it ever did."

"No, it doesn't. But there seems to be something real special about you. I haven't put my finger on it yet, but when I do, I'll tell you what I'm referring to."

No doubt, he was saying all the right things to me, stuff that I needed to hear, but trust me when I say I was no fool. He wanted something from me. I also wanted something from him. And after we had shared several more drinks and more laughter, I was ready to put it all on the line.

"Justin, why don't we get out of this noisy place and finish this conversation in a more private setting? Do you have a problem with that?"

He lifted his glass, then tossed the remainder of the alcohol down his throat. "I don't have a problem with that, and I thought you'd never ask. My question to you is, my place or yours?"

"Neither. Let's go somewhere and get a room."

Justin was all for it. We broke out of the restaurant like two bats coming from hell. Several hotels were close by the stadium, and when we entered the lobby of one of them, Justin went right to the counter and paid for a room. Things got a little heated in the elevator when he swung in front of me and planted a soft kiss on my lips. My breasts rose against his chest, and after staring into his eyes, I opened my mouth wide and sucked his thin lips with mine. The juicy kiss left me as horny as ever, and when the elevator opened, I followed his sexy self to the room.

He used the key card to open the door, and the moment we entered the room, there was a rush to remove our clothes. We didn't get far before Justin pinned me against the door while he kissed my face and neck. He ground hard against me, and as I attempted to unzip his jeans, he pulled at my shirt, ripping it open. My breasts popped out, giving him a clear invitation to suck them.

"Mmm," he moaned while licking my nipples. By now I had his jeans lowered, and my hands were pressed into his tight and muscular ass. I couldn't believe what I was about to do with this young man, and I doubted that Trina or Evelyn would believe me. I wasn't exactly drunk, either—tipsy for sure, but definitely not drunk. He was, though. But he was absolutely in control.

He pulled his mouth away from my breasts, then took a few steps back to look at me as I stood there with my back still against the door. Not only did my shirt hang off my shoulders, revealing both breasts, but now my jeans were unbuttoned, showing my purple lace panties.

"I know your pussy is going to be good," he said. "How in the hell did I get so lucky?"

When he kicked off his jeans and pulled his shirt over his head, I wondered the same thing. His package was mouthwatering. I couldn't believe the thickness of that thing, and the width of it made me a little nervous. I watched as he eased on a condom, and then he reached forward to secure my waist. He pulled me on the bed with him, and the first thing I did was give him a ride. I could feel my coochie being stretched far apart as I slowly guided myself up and down on him.

"And . . . and you have the nerve to rave about me," I said. "This dick is so worthy of my time."

"Then take as much time as you need. It's yours."

I did as I was told and used my time wisely. Justin and I screwed around for hours. He twisted my body in every position he could think of, and my favorite had to be when he tackled the goodies from behind. One of his feet was on the floor; the other on the bed. I was bent over and could feel every inch of him working me over.

"I could do this with you every day for the rest of my life," he strained to say. "Your pussy is so warm and tight, just how I like it."

I liked the way he felt too, but this was not something that was going to happen every day. It was a one-night stand for me, and I truly didn't believe that he would have a problem with that. Meanwhile, I wasn't about to run from this feeling. Apparently, neither was he. We were both caught up in the moment.

With his dick still resting inside of me, he lifted me from the bed. My entire backside was against him, and my legs were straddled wide. He used his strength to hold me up. His fingers brushed against my clit, and he took several soft bites on the side of my neck. I was seconds away from coming again, and this time, he released his energy with me.

"Fuck!" he shouted while thrusting faster inside of me. "Where in the hell did you come from?"

I should have asked him the same thing too, but I was too busy biting down on my lip to calm the feeling. I felt my juices flow all over him. His dick thumped inside of me, and just so we wouldn't hit the floor, we both crashed on the bed. I could feel Justin's heart beating fast against my back. His rock-solid body was covered in sweat, which dripped on me as I lay underneath him. I had been sweating too, and when he suggested a shower, we found ourselves doing the nasty in there too. He had me up in the air, with my back pinned against the wall. My legs straddled his waist, and for whatever reason, I just couldn't get enough.

"Damn you, Justin," I whispered. "I'm not supposed to be doing this with you. I don't do this kind of stuff, but it sure in the hell makes me regret that I didn't step out of the box sooner."

"I believe you about not doing this with anybody. I'm just glad you decided to do this with me."

Enough said, enough done. We wrapped up our sex session almost an hour later. Justin was beat, and he fell asleep. I quietly crawled out of bed, looked for my clothes. After giving him a sweet little kiss on his cheek, I jetted.

I left the hotel on a serious high. I couldn't wait to tell Trina and Evelyn about my little adventurous night with Justin, and I wanted to let them know that there was still some hope for me. Trina didn't answer her phone, and when I drove by her house, it was pitch black inside. I didn't want to wake her and Keith, so I made my way to Evelyn's place. To my surprise, when I swerved into a parking spot, I saw a car that I knew all too well. It was Cedric's car. Why in the hell would he be parked outside of her complex if he wasn't inside with Evelyn? My heart dropped to my stomach. I started to feel ill. I knew that trusting that hoochie again had been the wrong thing to do. And even though I felt so much hurt inside, I refused to go to the door and confront them. I just wasn't going there again, and at this point, I thought, *To hell with them both*. They could have each other, and they deserved to be together.

The second I got home, I did the norm and went straight to the liquor cabinet. Almost a whole bottle of vodka was there, and you'd better believe that I tore into it. I didn't want Jacoby to see me, so I made my way down the hallway and into my bedroom. I plopped on the bed, turned the bottle up to my lips, and thoroughly enjoyed my new fix.

7

Evelyn

Cedric and I were to the point where all we did was argue. I wholeheartedly regretted having had sex with him again, and after being at Kayla's house and seeing how torn she was, I wasn't about to go through with telling Cedric anything. Yes, the information about Jacoby was damaging. Cedric needed to know, but he damn sure wasn't going to get any info from me. I was done with him. I continued to tell him that Kayla hadn't said a thing to me about Jacoby or him.

"Stop lying, Evelyn," he said while sitting comfortably in my living room. He was casually dressed in tan slacks and a peach shirt. His loafers had a shine, and so did his chocolate skin. It was late, so I was dressed in a pink, see-through pajama top that cut right at my thighs.

"I'm not lying to you, Cedric. She told me that she didn't trust me. Said that she was still bitter about what happened. I can't get the information you need, so you're going to have to think of another way to get it."

"You think so, huh? Now that you have a little change in your pocket, you feel as if you don't need me. You feel as if you don't have to come through for me, like I came through for you, right?"

"You're making me feel as if I made a deal with the devil. I can't tell you something that I don't know. If you want me to lie to you, I will. There is no way for me to force Kayla to have a conversation that she doesn't want to have. My suggestion to you is this. Go talk to her. Ask her about the letter you got from Paula that mentioned Jacoby. Maybe she'll tell you something. Anything that will help you make sense of all of this. I'm just getting to the point where I can't help you. I've done all that I can do, and when all is said and done, you did get a nice chunk of the money from Mr. and Mrs. Washington too."

"Fuck money!" he shouted. "I don't need no goddamned money! What I need is for you to step up and do what the fuck you told me you was gon' do! You're running out of time, and I've given you plenty of it. There will be consequences if you don't follow through, bitch, and I'm just being honest."

Like I'd told Kayla and Trina earlier, I was sick and tired of this. Tired of Cedric and his shit. And the name-calling was totally uncalled for. I stood, then walked to the door. With my hand on the knob, I turned to him.

"Cedric, please leave. I'm not doing this with you tonight. I'm tired as hell. I'll keep talking to Kayla, but I don't know what good it's going to do. And if she says something to me that may interest you, I'll be in touch."

While wringing his hands together, he slowly got off the sofa and stretched. He strutted my way with narrowed eyes, then stood close to me at the door.

"Since you can't seem to deliver on one thing, you will deliver on another. I've had a long day at work, and I need my dick sucked tonight. Bow down now, and watch your teeth."

I moved my head from side to side. "I'm not in the mood tonight. Go home to Joy and ask her to suck your dick. I'm sure she's wondering where you are, and your late nights in the streets probably concern her."

Catching me off guard, Cedric reached back, then brought his hand forward to slap the shit out of me. He slapped me so hard that my hair shifted to one side. I was also moved a few inches away from the door.

"Don't worry about what my woman can and will do for me at home. When I ask you to do something within reason for me, you'd better do it! Now, I've been real patient with yo' ass, Evelyn. Real patient. Stop with the games and give me a little something in return."

There was a time when I thought I was in love with Cedric. I had wanted to spend my life with him, have his children, and spend his money. Now I hated him. I hated everything about him, and his dick didn't move me one bit. I lifted my finger, pointing it near his face. A mean mug was on my face, and I spoke through clenched teeth.

"Don't you ever put your hands on me like that again! You got away with that shit once before, and now you think I'm down with it. I'm not, and trust me when I say if you do that shit again, I will cut your balls off, stuff them in your mouth, and watch you choke on them."

He smirked at my comment, and then gave a loud laugh. "I believe you, 'cause you are one bad bitch. But get on your knees and send me out this door with some kind of smile on my face. That's the least you can do after failing to give me the information I need. Maybe I do need to seek other alternatives. Tonight, though, I want some head, and I need some pussy. Joy is being kind of stingy with the goods. She suspects that I've been fucking someone else, but none of that matters. Her ass is on the way out the door real soon."

It wasn't as if he was doing me any favors by kicking her out. Cedric was a mess, but like always, in order to keep the peace, he got what he wanted from me. I didn't drop to my knees until we were in the bedroom, and as I held his package in my hand, I started to get him back for slapping me earlier. But now wasn't the time or the place. I locked my mouth on his shaft and sucked him until my jaws got tired. I had a headache from bobbing for so long, and I was thankful when I looked up and saw that he had fallen asleep. This was another opportunity for me to get back at him. It was such a shame that he underestimated me. He wasn't the only one who had done so, and I lay there thinking that it was time for me to pay Charles another visit.

Two days later I found out about a grand opening event that Charles was expected to attend later that day. A new technology company was opening in St. Louis, and the company Charles worked for was one of the big donors. This time around, I had to pretend that I wasn't there to see him. Basically, I was there for support, and plenty of people had been invited to come out and attend the all-white dress party to celebrate new jobs for our youth. I wasn't sure if his wife would join him or not, but her presence wouldn't bother me one bit. I was on a mission, and whenever I wanted something, nine times out of ten I got it. Money used to be the exception, but all I could say was, "Look at me now."

I spent the whole day looking for the perfect dress. My hair had already been done, and it was still dark blonde. It was similar to Beyoncé's, as were my curves. When I found a white dress that was sheer in some areas and covered with pearls and silk fabric in other areas, and had a plunging neckline and a long slit up the front, I suspected that Charles would rethink his position. The shoes I found were like Cinderella's glass slippers. The crystal-like heels were almost five inches, and there were tiny diamond studs near the front. I was pleased with the whole outfit, and when I got home to try on everything, I felt ready for Hollywood Boulevard.

I tucked my purse underneath my arm, grabbed my keys, then headed to the event in my new silver Mercedes. I arrived at the Renaissance Hotel almost an hour late. Traffic was a mess, and because I didn't want to be delayed any longer, I gave my keys to the valet and let the nice gentleman park my car. I headed to the ballroom where the event was being held, and right outside the door I saw groups of people dressed in white. I figured it would be difficult to find Charles, and I became totally convinced of this when I entered the ballroom and discovered that it was filled to capacity.

Several dressy round tables had been set up, a long buffet stretched from one corner of the room to the other, a band was playing music in another corner, and many of the people there were tuned in to a PowerPoint presentation that provided more information about the new technology company. I pretended to be tuned in too, especially since so many eyes were on me. Yes, there was a bunch of women standing around, hating, and none of them looked as good as I did in my dress. Several men nudged each other, and I saw one woman catch an attitude because her man kept looking in my direction. I guessed I was grateful to my mother for something. I definitely had her good looks. There was no question that she was, indeed, a beautiful woman. Too bad she didn't know how to take advantage of what God had blessed her with, and it was such a shame that she had allowed my father to use her until he couldn't do it anymore.

A little while later, along with everyone else, I waited in a long line to get some food. I started to converse with two ladies who stood in line with me, and then I joined them, along with several others, at one of the round tables.

"Ooh, your hair is so pretty," the older woman said, touching my hair. "How do you get all that body and bounce? I've been trying to get my hair like that for years."

She didn't have to put her hands in my hair, but I didn't mind telling her my secret. "I use Shea Moisture and several products from Carol's Daughter. I don't remember the specific names of the products, but I'm sure they'll come to mind before I leave."

"Let me know too," said a woman who was sitting across the table from us and who had a thirsty-looking weave on. I ignored her because there wasn't a product on the market that would help her hair look like mine.

For the next several minutes, I got my grub on and chatted with the women and the men at our table. The room filled up even more, and when I saw some of the VIPs take a seat up front, that was when I spotted Charles. My mouth dropped open. When I said he was sexy as hell, I truly meant it. The white tailored tuxedo he wore set his black ass off. Keith and Bryson didn't have shit on ole dad, and judging by the way he strutted around and flashed his Crest smile, he knew he was all that. I searched the room, looking for Netta. There wasn't a chance in hell that she had let him attend an event like this alone. If she was as supportive as he said she was, I was sure she was somewhere lurking in the crowd. As I sat there in a trance from looking at him, I felt a hot breath next to my ear.

"Do you mind if I ask you to step outside in the hallway so we can talk?"

I snapped my head to the side, only to see a brotha with long dreads and too much facial hair standing next to me. He was cute, but not cute enough to steal my attention away from Charles.

"Maybe later," I said. "I'd really like to hear what's going on, and I think some of the VIPs are about to speak."

"Sure," he said. "You're looking good, girl, and I for sure want to catch up with you later."

Damn. Was this some kind of club or something? The men sure did make it seem that way, even though everyone there was supposed to be there to support our youth. I had other reasons for being there, but that was just me.

Two proper-talking women went to the podium and spoke first. I was waiting for them to go sit down somewhere. Some people always liked to appear important, and trust me when I say that there were enough women flouncing around in white, off white, and dirty white, trying to get attention. I didn't have to put myself there, and sitting right where I was, which was in the front, provided me with all the attention I needed, especially when Charles stepped to the podium and gave his little spiel about donating. The first person his eyes connected with was me. He squinted just to be sure that it was me. Then he turned his head in the other direction.

The hot and bothered, nosy woman next to me had to open her big mouth. "Why does he keep looking at you like that? Do you know him?"

"Uh, no, I don't. But he sure is good to look at, isn't he?"

"Girl, you ain't said nothing but a word. He could lay me on my back right here and right now. I would certainly enjoy that."

Another woman quickly chimed in. "Mr. Washington is a married man. God don't like ugly, and there is no need for y'all to sit there and disrespect his wife. After all, he who finds a wife finds a good thing and obtains favor from the Lord."

Huh? How did we manage to switch from here to church? The woman next to me let that Bible-thumping heifer have it before I did.

"How are we disrespecting his wife by paying him a compliment? You need to hush your doggone mouth and go somewhere with that."

"Exactly," I said, rolling my eyes and keeping it short.

"I'm not gon' hush, and when you're talking about lying on your back, you are disrespecting his wife. I'm not going to sit here and argue with y'all, either, and both of you bitches can burn in hell."

I just shook my head and laughed at the wannabe Christian woman. She needed Jesus way more than I did. She was so upset that when we continued to talk about Charles, she got up, intent on moving elsewhere. She mumbled something under her breath as she turned to leave, and that was when the lady next to me at the table got louder.

"We can have this conversation outside," she informed the wannabe Christian woman. "Just tell me when you're ready to go."

The woman rolled her eyes, then walked away. I couldn't believe it was that serious for her.

"She didn't want none of this. Some people are nuts," the woman next to me said. "She needed to mind her own business, and if we're going to burn in hell, that's for Jesus to decide."

I hit her with another "Exactly," then got back to watching Charles.

It was a good thing that the band was still softly playing music and that the PowerPoint presentation was still keeping many people occupied. Charles was still speaking, but I ignored pretty much everything he said. I focused on those sexy lips, and every time he licked them, I felt a jab in my pussy. I looked at his big hands and visualized them touching my body. His dick print was on point, and when he stepped away from the podium for a few minutes, I got a clear glimpse of it. Most of the women in the audience looked like zombies and seemed to be in a trance, as I was. Their eyes were glued to him, and I was 120 percent positive that I wasn't the only woman in the room with dirty thoughts in her head.

"So we're very excited about this new venture," he said. "And I welcome all of you, each and every one of you, to get behind this company and watch our youth grow."

Applause erupted. Before walking away from the podium, Charles took one last glance at me. The music kicked up again, and numerous people rushed over to the buffet line to get more food. Charles made his way through the crowd, but he was stopped by so many people who wanted to talk, mostly men who sat in the VIP section. I saw several of them step into the wide hallway with him. That was when I got up and proceeded to make my move.

Displaying much confidence, I paraded down the hallway with my head held high. My hips swayed like Olivia Pope's from *Scandal*, and my heels clacked on the floor. From a distance, I could see several of the men who were standing with Charles look my way. And the one thing I knew about men was that they loved to compete. They loved attention, and for me to give it to just one, I knew that one would feel special. The others would stand there with jealousy in their eyes, wondering why they weren't the chosen one.

As I approached the VIP circle of men, they began to part like the Red Sea. Heads turned, eyes zoomed in, and many of them wet their lips. Charles turned around too, and as soon as I walked by him, as if it was in the plan, a thirsty man spoke up.

"Slow down, beautiful, and drop your name on me," he said.

"Forget it, man. She don't seem like the kind of woman who would be interested in you. Maybe I need to introduce myself instead," another man declared.

They laughed, and I stopped to flash a smile.

"Evelyn," I said while observing some of the wealthy black men in my presence. I could smell the money, but only one of them was of great interest to me. "My name is Evelyn, and I am really happy to be here. I love what you all are doing for our youth, and, Mr. Washington, the speech you gave was simply amazing."

He was the only one who wasn't smiling. I didn't want to entertain his little attitude right now, so I hurried to wrap this up.

"Gentlemen, please enjoy the evening. And thanks a million for the compliments."

I strutted away, knowing for a fact that every last one of their eyes was on my backside. I had no panties on, and I was sure someone, maybe even Charles, had noticed. I went into the ladies' room to check myself in the mirror. "Fucking fabulous" was written all over me. I washed my hands, dried them with a paper towel, and then left. As I made my exit, I ran right into Charles, who stood close to the door. His hands were in his pockets, and that same blank expression was on his face.

"Wha-what do you want from me, Evelyn? Is this how it's going to be? Are you going to keep showing up at places where you know I'll be, until I give you some attention?"

I kept it real with him. "You already know what I want, so no need to ask. And if you think I'm some kind of stalker, please rethink your thoughts. I'm here with a friend of mine tonight. He invited me to attend this special occasion with him. I had no idea you would be here, and quite frankly, I was shocked to see you. Now, if you don't mind, I need to go back inside the ballroom. I've been gone for a while, and I'm sure my friend is looking for me."

I attempted to walk away, but he snatched me by the arm. I looked at his hand tightly squeezing my arm, then shifted my eyes to his. He stared me down, then lifted his other arm to look at his gold watch.

"One hour," he said. "In one hour meet me out front. You'll recognize what kind of car I'm in, and if you're not there in an hour, I'm leaving."

I didn't bother to reply. When he let go of my arm, I turned around and proceeded to walk, with a slight smirk on my face. All I could think to myself was, *Got him*.

I pranced around the ballroom, talking to people whom I did not know. Some of the conversations were interesting, but many were stirred up to waste time. And before I knew it, the long hand hit twelve and my hour was up. I said a few good-byes, exchanged numbers with several people, and promised this one lady whom I had been talking to that I would make a donation to her organization. After that, I walked outside. Sitting behind the steering wheel of a muthafucking Maybach was Charles. Dark shades covered his eyes, and with the slightly tinted windows, I could barely see him. I walked his way, and he unlocked the passenger door so I could get inside the car.

"Hurry up and close the door," he said.

I shut the door, giving us all the privacy we needed. The soft leather seats were so comfortable that I felt as if my body was melting. I had never ridden in one of these cars before, and this was something special.

"Here's the deal," Charles said with arrogance. "I give you what you want, and I never want to see your face again. I thought that I'd already taken care of you, but obviously not. I don't want you to mention anything about Bryson, and please don't say anything about my wife. Got it?"

"I clearly do, but don't sit there and pretend that you're giving me everything that I want, when you know darn well that this is something that you want too."

"Do I need to repeat what I just said?"

"No. And like I said . . . nice car."

For the first time, Charles smiled. "Good girl," he said. Then he sped off.

I wasn't sure where we were headed, but it looked to me as if we were heading toward his office. He was speeding like crazy, and as we drove by many cars, people were trying to get a peek at who was inside his. Once we hit the highway, Charles tore it up. That was until we saw flashing lights behind us. He pulled over, and I watched through the side mirror as the cop got out of the car.

"You are in major trouble," I said playfully. "And don't ask me to help you pay that ticket, because it's going to be very expensive."

"I assure you that I won't be getting any tickets today."

"Would you like to put some money on that? I don't care how much you're worth. Your skin is still black."

Charles lowered the window to address the officer. The first thing the officer did was peek into the car.

"License, insurance, and registration, please."

"For what?" Charles said.

"You were speeding. Fast."

"No I wasn't. What I was doing was trying to keep up with the flow of traffic."

"You were way ahead of traffic. Now again, I need to see your license, insurance, and registration."

Charles tapped a button that opened a small compartment between us. He pulled out his license, then gave it to the officer. "I don't have my insurance card on me, and my registration is in another vehicle. See what you can do to work with that."

The officer took his license and then bent down to look at me again. "Good evening, ma'am," he said. "What's your name, and can I get some identification from you too?"

I reached for my purse, but Charles reached over and touched my hands. "You don't need any identification from her. She's not driving this car. I am."

I didn't want no shit, but it seemed to me as if Charles knew something that I didn't.

The officer walked away with a slightly red face. I could tell he was pissed.

"See? You done really made him mad. He's going to write you several tickets. And why would you not carry your insurance and registration papers with you?"

"My insurance and registration papers are right in this car. And I would have given them to him had he not approached my car with an attitude," Charles replied, raising his window.

The officer came back in less than two or three minutes. Charles lowered the window again, and the officer handed him his license back.

"Have a good evening, sir. And slow it down a bit."

"Will do," was all Charles said, and then he looked both ways before taking off.

"Hold up," I said. "What in the hell just happened back there? You were supposed to get a ticket. But all you got was a 'Have a good evening, sir.'"

"Hey. Some of us got it, and some of us don't. They definitely know who does, and that's all I'm going to say about that."

It left me pretty speechless too. I did, however, talk to Charles about Keith and Trina. He didn't tell me that I couldn't say anything about them. And all I asked was if he liked Trina and if he thought she would one day be his daughter-in-law.

"That's for Keith to decide, not me. I don't have an opinion about her one way or the other."

"Do you think she's cute? She's a good friend of mine, but I promise not to tell her if you think she's cute enough for your son."

"If my son thinks she's cute, that's all that matters."

"Do you expect me to believe that you don't have any influence on your sons and their relationships? I don't believe that for one minute, Charles. To me, it seems like you're the kind of father who can say, 'Jump,' and they respond, 'How high?' Bryson is spoiled by his mother, not you. Am I right?"

"See, I asked you not to go there. I don't discuss my family with strangers, so let it go and focus on something else."

"I'm real focused. Focused on what I want and what I intend to get from this one night. The one thing that I would like for you to tell me is if you're hard already or if you got a sock in your pants that's making your *thingy* down there look massive."

Charles didn't want to laugh, but he did. Shook his head, too, and then pulled into the parking garage at his office building. He turned to me with his index finger pressed against his temple.

"How can you say something like that to a grown-ass man? And for the record, the only socks I have on me are on my feet. You're a mess, Evelyn, but there's something intriguing about you that I like. And even though I like it, I don't want no parts of it after today. Promise me that you won't continue to pursue me."

"I'm bad with promises, and I often break them. Besides, even if I did make you that promise, you wouldn't believe me."

"No, I wouldn't. But I will make you a promise that I intend to keep. If my wife or sons ever find out about this one-night adventure, I will, indeed, make you disappear."

I ran my fingers across my lips, zipping them. "Your secret is safe with me."

I followed Charles inside the building, but instead of going up in the elevator, we went down. Down into the basement, which made me a little nervous. For a minute, I thought he was tricking me. I also thought he was going to do something horrible to me, until we stopped in front of another door, which prompted him to provide a code. Charles quickly punched in a few numbers, and the door slid open. I didn't know where in the hell we were, and I couldn't believe this Negro had some kind of underground bunker that was set up like a real apartment. That made me even more nervous, and I hoped that he wouldn't break out with any *Fifty Shades* bullshit. I wasn't into whips or chains. Just didn't get down like that, though I meant no offense to people who did.

I watched as Charles entered another code, which secured the door behind us. Talk about a nigga being discreet . . . He definitely was and then some. I was sure that Netta had no idea about this place. And that was why I didn't buy that bullshit about him loving his wife and never betraying her. Most men with money, like Charles, did what the hell they wanted to. There wasn't enough love in the world to stop them from delving into a piece of pussy if they desired it.

"Well, well, well," I said, looking around at the spacious area that was hooked up like some shit right out of a James Bond movie. There was a lounging area, a bar area, and a section that had a Jacuzzi and a TV. A small boardroom was behind a wide expanse of glass, and a beautiful aquarium surrounded the entire space. If I told anybody about this, they wouldn't believe me. Cameras were everywhere, and I also saw a room that monitored several different places. I had no idea what those places were, but as I began to look harder, Charles picked up a remote and shut that room down, turning it pitch black.

"Let me guess," I said. "CIA, right?"

"No. RTF," he replied, then took off his suit jacket and tossed it on a leather circular sofa.

"It will take forever for me to figure that out, and I think I may need some help."

"Yes, you do."

He stepped forward to remove my dress. After moving the top of it away from my shoulders and exposing my breasts, he asked me to turn around so he could unzip it. I did so, and when my dress fell to my ankles, I stood naked. He walked in a circle, observing every inch of my body as I stood there.

"Flawless," he said, stopping in his tracks. "Unquestionably flawless, and I am so RTF."

It took me a minute, but as he grabbed a nice chuck of my ass and shook it, I finally got it. "I'm ready to fuck too. Lead the way and allow me to serve you."

Charles took my hand and directed me down a short hallway that led to a bedroom. I stood in awe as I looked at the huge round bed that was fit for a king. I honestly did not know what in the hell this man did, but I had to admit that it felt good being in his presence. The whole room was shaped like a circle. The bed sat elevated in the center of the room, and a spacious tub was to my right. To the left was a curved TV, and another bar area was beside it. An open shower was visible too. Glass surrounded it, and it was large enough for at least twenty people to stand inside it. This was so breathtaking, and as I stood with a shocked look on my face, Charles crept up behind me. He massaged my breasts together, and I couldn't even explain what the feeling of his gentle hands was doing to me.

"What are you thinking?" he whispered in my ear. "About my sock?"

I laughed, but trust me when I say that it was no laughing matter when he dimmed the lights, removed his clothes, laid me on that bed, and introduced me to his sock. I had never in my life tampered with a dick so big. I had to back away from that thing, because I thought he was trying to slip something else inside me.

"Wait a minute," I said, scooting back. "What is that?"

Charles stood with pride. My eyes traveled to his package, and all I could say to myself was, *Lord, have mercy on me*. I had never witnessed anything like it. He planned to rupture my insides with that motherfucker. I quickly had second thoughts about this.

"Listen," I said while sitting up on the bed, "I don't know if I'm ready for this. You are not about to put all of that in me. I assure you that it won't fit, and if it won't fit, I must acquit."

"I'm not going to let you do that, because you went through so much trouble to get me here. And now that I'm here, you don't want it? The least you can do is try to work with it. As creative as you are, I'm sure you can come up with something to help you cope."

I had a feeling that this was the end of my sex life. A dick that size could damage me for life. Nonetheless, after he put on a condom, I took my chances. I allowed Charles to take it real slow, but after he journeyed eleven or twelve inches deep, I couldn't even move. My whole body stiffened. My pussy felt as if it was being stretched far, far apart. How in the hell was Netta able to handle all of this? She was brave, and I had to give her props. How could she have had two kids by this man, and why had she agreed to spend the rest of her life with him? This was too much! He kept planting soft kisses on my neck to calm me, but those kisses didn't do much good. I touched his chest to push him back.

"I—I can't do this. As much as I want to, I have to admit that I am *way* out of your league."

Frustration was written all over Charles's face. "Stop talking about what you can't do, and show me what you can do. I'm going to ease it out and let you take control of this. Whatever you do, don't waste my time. Please. And thank you."

Well, since he had put it like that, I put my big girl panties on and did my best to take control. I started by getting on top of Charles. My legs straddled him, and as I looked between my legs, I could see his long, hard pipe, which damn near surpassed the top of my breasts. My wet coochie lips coated one side of his shaft, and when I was ready to take in a few inches, I lifted myself up high. One inch went in, then two. Two turned into five; then five switched to ten. He was about twelve inches deep again when I started to feel the pain.

"Don't get greedy," he said, helping to guide me. "Take it easy, and after a few more inches, you'll be just fine."

Shit. Not in this lifetime. I worked with what I could for a while, and I doubted that I would be able to take him all in. My pussy was sore as fuck. Even though his strokes felt nice, it was very difficult to enjoy a man this size. I could hurt myself by chasing this dick, and I now knew why this room was in a bunker, where no one could hear. Any woman who was brave enough to come down here and fuck him had to scream and holler. There was no way to stay silent, and as I moved up and down on him, my mouth stayed open. I had to catch my breath after spewing words like "shit," "fuck," and "damn." Every time I made a safe landing, there I was, singing vowels and saying words that echoed loudly in the room.

"Ooh, mmm, aahhh, noooo. Please don't move, and give me a minute."

As Charles halted his thrusts inside me, I remained still. I released several deep breaths; then I tackled him again.

"Aahhh, yesss, yes, baby, yes! I think I'm ready for more!" I yelled.

Charles lifted his hand and covered my mouth. "Let's try something different," he said. "You may not like the idea of it, but it's going to help you get through this a lot easier." He removed his hand from my mouth.

"I don't know what else I can do, but I'm listening," I said.

"Allow me to secure your arms and legs. That way you can't stop me. You won't be able to prevent me from doing all that I want to do to you, and all we have is a few more hours together. Why not take advantage of the time and enjoy ourselves a bit more?"

I was hesitant, but what the hell? You only lived once, and I was eager to get to a point where I could thoroughly enjoy this. I held my arms together in front of me.

"Secure me. And try like hell not to hurt me."

I slid off Charles and watched as he got off the bed and went into another room. He came back with four ropes, which he used to tie my wrists to the bed, and with my legs spread wide, he tied my ankles.

"You can get loose if you struggle hard enough, but please don't try too hard. I want you to withstand as much pain as you can, and then you will discover how much easier this will be."

This time, Charles lay on top of me and pecked my lips, giving me a soft kiss. I wanted to rub the back of his head, but I couldn't. I also wanted another kiss, so I lifted my head and stuck my tongue into his mouth. The kiss was all of that and then some. I didn't know why he held back on me, but it definitely relaxed me. So did the feel of his tongue as he licked down my neck, journeyed between my breasts, and landed in my belly button. He entertained that spot for only a few minutes, and then his tongue turned up the heat in my pussy. A very high arch formed in my back; then I pulled tightly on the ropes. The feeling was so intense that I attempted to free my legs so I could wrap them around him.

"Oh, my *God*," I said, squirming around. "Help me, *please*."

Charles backed his tongue out of me, making sure I was soaking wet. He turned the tip of his thick head against my hole, as if he were about to screw it in. The feel of it made me tremble all over, and without breaking down his insertions so that he went inch by inch, he rammed the whole thing inside me. My whole body jerked forward. My stomach was in so much pain. I let out a scream that was sure to bust his eardrums. Tears ran from the corners of my eyes. That was when he leaned in and planted a soft kiss on my cheek.

"Warning," he said. "I need to do that again."

He backed out and went full force again and again. I grunted loudly after each thrust and tugged at the ropes to attempt to free myself. No such luck. He repeated his actions, and each time he went in, it felt like I was being operated on without being given anesthesia. His dick touched something in my body that I didn't know was there. But eventually, it started to feel real good to me. My grunts got softer and softer, and my pussy juices rained on him like never before.

"I told you, you could handle this," he said while rubbing my trembling legs. "It's in there, baby, all the way in there, and there's no need to fuss anymore. Relax and let your legs fall apart so I can give you what you wished for."

Charles gave me just that—a good ole dick beating, along with multiple orgasms. His strokes started off smooth and slow, but as things started to loosen up more, he didn't hold back. My sweaty body squirmed all over the bed, and several times I fought hard to jump off it. The ropes helped to keep me in place. And after almost twenty minutes of being beat down by his penis, I finally felt some relief. I ground right along with him. Locked my coochie on his muscle and didn't want to let go. When he freed my hands, I got on my hands and knees to show him just how courageous I was. But no matter how hard I tried to please him, he wound up defeating me. Broke my pussy down to an all new low. Had me spewing made-up words that were no part of the English language. I couldn't be mad, because I had asked for this, all of it, and he'd given me that and then some.

At almost four in the morning, it was over. Done. Complete. And there was never supposed to be seconds. I could barely walk. Pussy felt loose, and my back hurt like hell. Charles walked behind me as we made our way back to his car.

"I know a good doctor you can go to, if you need one," he said in a playful manner.

I was exhausted and barely had enough strength to laugh at his joke. "No, thank you. Keep your doctor, and you can keep that dick too. I won't be needing anything else like that for at least another year or two from now."

"I doubt that, and all I will say about that is we'll see."

We got into his car, and almost forty-five minutes later, we were back at the hotel. He dropped me off so I could get my car and go on my merry little way. As I slowly exited his car, he reached for my arm.

"Damn. A man can't have one last kiss before you go? You shouldn't even be like that, especially after all that I gave you tonight."

I could barely lean in for a kiss. It was a quick one too, and so was my final good-bye. I waved at him, then shut the door. Walked slowly to my car, drove slowly home, and took a long, hot bath when I got there. I damn near fell asleep while closing my eyes and thinking about this night, which I would never forget. Too bad I couldn't share it with my BFF's. Trina, for sure, would kill me.

8

Trina

It was so easy to say one thing yet do another. I had been on the phone with Sasha again. She'd called me the other day, in tears. I couldn't ignore her calls. During our conversation, she had asked if I would come see her. Said that it wasn't solely because she wanted to see me, but that she also wanted to get me some money, which I so desperately needed. I wanted to tell Keith, but then again I didn't. I knew how he would react, and I had been doing my best to prevent any arguments with him. He still seemed on edge about some of the things that were going on with his family, and in order to clear his head, he was spending more time painting and going to the gym. He had also started hanging out with some friends of his, but since he always invited me to go, I didn't trip. He had come in at around three in the morning last night. And I had just gotten off the phone with Sasha. I had pretended to be asleep, so he hadn't bothered me.

The next morning, while Keith was still resting, I searched for airline tickets on the Internet. Sasha had asked me to come to New York soon, so I checked the prices to see which day was the best one to go. I found a good deal for this Thursday, for a flight departing St. Louis at eleven and arriving in New York at a little after three. There was a deal on hotels too, so I search for one that was close to where Sasha lived. I didn't think it would be appropriate for me to stay with her, especially since she already had a girlfriend. And if things didn't pan out like I intended them to, I could always go back to the hotel, pack, and bring my tail back home. Without further ado, I booked the flight and paid for three nights at the hotel. I didn't have a lot of money in my account, so I pulled a few hundred dollars from Keith's account and put it into mine. I did that often, and I was sure that he wouldn't trip.

After booking my trip, I called Kayla to check on her. She had been calling me, but every time I called her back, she didn't answer her phone. I had started to go by her condo to check on her, and I would do so if she didn't answer this time around. Thankfully, she did.

"Girl, where have you been?" I said.

"Here and there. At the movies, at Jacoby's school, over at his girlfriend's house, and in a hotel room with a young white man who showed me what I've been missing out on."

"What? Stop playing. And something like that would happen only in your dreams."

"I am very serious. You know I wouldn't lie to you about anything like that."

"You sound serious, but what made you go there? I've never known you to just up and have sex with someone you barely know."

"Well, sometimes you get tired of the same ole, same ole. I wanted to explore something different, and I'm glad I did."

"I can't be mad at you for that, and I hope it was good to you."

"It was, and you won't hear any complaints from me."

"Anything serious brewing? Have you spoken to him again or not?"

"Nope. But I'm good with that. I don't need the hassles, and there are times when I prefer to be alone."

"I know you do, but on another note, how have you been doing with the drinking thing? Be honest, Kayla, and you know I can tell when you be lying to me."

"The truth is . . . I've been doing okay. Not drinking as much as I was, but I've still been drinking here and there. The key is to keep myself busy and stop worrying so much. I also realized that there are certain things that I can't change, and that refers to other people too. I stopped by your place the other night to tell you about the guy I met. It looked like you and Keith were asleep, because the whole house was dark. I left your place and went to Evelyn's. You're not going to believe whose car was parked outside."

I pondered this for a quick second and then stared at the bookshelf in front of me in disbelief. "Please don't tell me Cedric was over there."

"Yes, he was. It took everything in me not to go to the door, but then I asked myself what for. He's not my husband anymore, and he's free to screw around with whomever. If Evelyn is who he wants, so be it. I don't have much else to say to her, because I'm sick and tired of being played like a fool and lied to. I thought she was sincere this time, and more than anything, I thought she had learned a valuable lesson."

Hearing Kayla tell me this just broke my heart. I had thought the same thing too. I didn't think Evelyn was that in love with Cedric, but maybe she was. Maybe he was in love with her too, and neither of them knew how to come clean about their feelings. This was so messed up. I really didn't know what to say to Kayla. Never again would I ask her to forgive Evelyn.

"I'm glad you're not taking this too hard. And I feel bad for forcing you to move on from the past when she keeps slapping you in the face."

"That's all I'm saying. And you didn't force me to do anything. I thought that forgiving her was the right thing to do, but sometimes you just have to let go."

We both agreed on that. I asked Kayla if or when she planned on telling Cedric about the situation with Jacoby. With her spilling her guts to me and Evelyn, we knew it was just a matter of time before she ran back and told him everything.

"I've been thinking about that too," she said. "Jacoby's been bugging me about allowing him to explain the situation to Cedric, but I just don't know. It looks like that conversation may have to take place real soon, and to be honest, I've already been searching for an attorney to represent him."

"That's good. If I can do anything to help, let me know. Keith's parents know a lot of people, and I don't mind reaching out to them and asking for their help. I don't know how his mother is feeling about me these days, but I'll do whatever to help."

"What happened between you and Keith's mother? I thought she liked you."

I explained to Kayla what Evelyn had done while she was over there, trying to settle things between herself and Bryson. Kayla didn't have anything nice to say about it.

"Trina, you are too darn nice. How much damage are you going to let her do to you? That kind of mess didn't slip, and she intentionally said that to tell your business and put you on blast. She doesn't want his parents to like you. It was her way of making sure his mother views you in a different light."

"I never know what Evelyn's intentions are, but if his mother holds that against me, then she never liked me, anyway. I haven't spoken to her since then. Normally, she calls to check on me and Keith, but she's been reaching out to him on his cell phone, instead of calling the home phone."

"How do you know she calls on his cell phone, and why are you checking his messages? Only insecure women do that, and please don't tell me that you have a reason to be insecure."

"I don't, but I do look at his calls from time to time. A woman can never be too sure, and after all that has happened, you know how difficult it is for me to trust anyone. There are times when I don't even trust myself."

"I know exactly what you mean. But tell Keith I said hello, and if his mother doesn't call you, call her. Don't let Evelyn's nonsense come between y'all."

I told Kayla I would call Keith's mother, but a huge part of me was afraid to. Netta was good at reading people, and I didn't want her to question me about my experiences with women. I would wait to make that call. After Kayla and I hung up, I made a mental note to contact Evelyn about what Kayla had told me. The fact that she was screwing Cedric again was a big disappointment. It was yet another blow to our friendship.

Keith woke up around noon. I was upstairs, sketching a picture on a small canvas, which I intended to ship to Sasha before I left.

"I'm going outside to cut the grass," he said. "Maybe we can go to the movies or something later. I want to check out that new comedy movie, and if anybody needs a good laugh, it's me." He looked tired, and it also seemed that he had something weighing heavily on his mind.

"What's wrong? Do you want to talk about it? If so, you know I'm here."

"I know, but I don't want to discuss it right now. I get tired of talking about my family, and one of these days, I'm going to move away from here and be done with everything. You gon' move with me, aren't you?"

"Where you go, I go. I'm riding this out with you all the way to the end."

Keith walked farther into the room to give me a kiss. He then left the room and headed outside to cut the grass. I felt horrible inside. I knew that I was about to lie to him—I was going to tell him that Evelyn, Kayla, and I were going to take a trip somewhere together—and I decided to wait until later to do it. While he was outside, I called Kayla back to make sure she would cover for me, just in case.

"What? Why are you lying to that man like that? And where exactly are you going?"

"I'll tell you all about it another day. Right now I'm going outside to help my man cut the grass."

"Please do call me back. I want to know what is up with you."

I told Kayla that I would call her later, but just like when I spilled my guts to Evelyn, I feared being judged. Some people just didn't understand how difficult it was when you just hadn't discovered yet who you were or who exactly you wanted to be with. It was a scary feeling to know that loving someone just wasn't enough to fill the slightest void inside.

I put on my sweat suit and went outside to help Keith cut the grass. Afterward, we showered together, indulged in a quickie, and then went to dinner at Applebee's. During dinner I finally told him about the fabricated trip I was taking to Las Vegas with Kayla and Evelyn. He seemed okay with it, and I was shocked that he didn't even gripe about me going with Evelyn.

"You must have something really heavy on your mind," I said. "I can't believe that you didn't complain about me going somewhere with Evelyn."

"I don't have time for Evelyn right now. Besides, all I want is for you to have a good time. You need to get away, and I'm happy that you'll be spending some time with your friends. Maybe this is what y'all need."

"Maybe so, but what about you? Are you ready to tell me about what is bothering you? I don't know why you always try to keep things about your family a secret. You know you can talk to me about anything."

"I do, but some family matters have to stay in the family. When you become my wife, then I'll tell you."

I smiled. "Is that a proposal?"

Keith scooted close to me, then wrapped his arm around my waist. "No, it's not, but I assure you that it's coming." He pecked my lips, then rubbed my nose with his. I swore that I loved this man. I truly did, but it was difficult to express what I was going through.

"You say it's coming, but I have a little feeling that your mother is trying to stop you. Am I right, and are her comments about me starting to bug you? I noticed that she hasn't called me ever since Evelyn told her about me. And I also know that she's been in touch with you."

Keith released his arm from my waist. "I have to be honest with you about this, so yes, she has been making comments that I don't approve of. But my mother is set in her ways. I can't do anything about that. She has these issues with you, but what she needs to do is have a real talk with her son. Bryson continues to lie to her, and just the other day, I got a call from his daughter's mother, telling me some crap about what he did to her while they were in London. He's out of control. I don't know what it's going to take for my parents to stand up and put him in his place."

"Bryson is a grown man, Keith. You all speak about him like he's some kind of teenager. Your parents have no control over what he does, and if that's how he wants to live his life, so be it. His girlfriend shouldn't be calling you or anyone else. She has put up with his mess for a long time, and what she needs to do is end it. I don't get why so many women stay in abusive relationships like that. She knows that he goes both ways too, and I guess she's in denial, like he is."

"All of that could be true, but it still doesn't stop my mother from calling me and crying about it. She's upset about not seeing her only grandchild, and I'll sure be glad when we have a baby. I really want you to stop taking your pills. Are you ready to have a baby with me, or would you prefer to be my wife before we venture there?"

I almost choked on the water I was drinking. This was a conversation that I wasn't looking forward to having. Of course I wanted to have his baby, and one day I wanted to be his wife. Now . . . today I wasn't ready for that. I didn't know how to say it, but I replied in a way that I didn't think would offend him.

"I want to have your baby, but you know I have to get myself together financially. I don't want to depend on you for everything, and you need a wife who has a solid career and who can contribute to the marriage."

"Money is not an issue, and you already know that. I don't care if you contribute one dime, and there are other ways that you can contribute without dishing out money. It may be years before you feel as if your career is solid. The art industry is a tough business, and it took me almost eleven years before I started to make some decent money on my paintings."

Damn. Why did he have to go there with this? I was forced into a conversation that required me to be on the defensive.

"Money isn't an issue for you, but it is for me. And while I know you can and will provide for us, I still want to contribute more than good pussy. I have no desire to be barefoot and in the kitchen with a lot of babies. That's not me, and I think you already know that. At the moment, it's easy for you to make ten or fifteen thousand dollars on one painting. I'm not there yet, but I'm trying to get there too. Just be patient with me. In time you will have everything you want, and so will I."

Keith didn't reply. He picked up a buffalo wing, then bit into it. After tossing back another drink, he said he was ready to go home. The movies were squashed, and we spent the rest of our evening watching TV and not saying much at all to each other.

9

Kayla

I had put the bottle of alcohol down and had got serious, especially after seeing Cedric's car at Evelyn's place. She had left several messages for me, but I had ignored all of them. Instead, I had got motivated to deal with this situation with Jacoby and come up with the best solution. I didn't want to waste much more time on this, and I had a feeling that it would be just a matter of time before the police were knocking at my door to take my son away. Thanks to Evelyn.

Last night Jacoby and I had spoken to a lawyer, who had seemed very helpful. He had encouraged us to do our best to work this out with Cedric. "The truth," he'd said, "will set you free," so I had decided to invite Cedric over and let Jacoby tell him what he'd done while the two of them were in my presence.

After Jacoby got out of school and was done with band practice, I called Cedric at work. He sounded as if he was busy, so I hurried to tell him the purpose for my call.

"Jacoby and I need to talk to you about something very important. If you can come over after work, I would appreciate it very much."

"I don't mind coming over, but it may be around six or seven. Do you care to tell me what this is about?"

"I will once you get here."

"I don't like surprises, Kayla. Did Jacoby tell you why he has distanced himself from me, or are you going to tell me that I'm going to be a grandfather? I'm not ready to be one of those yet, and you need to stop him from spending so much time with Adrianne."

There he was again, telling me what I needed to do. I rolled my eyes, then sighed. "No, you're not going to be a grandfather, and I love his relationship with Adrianne. She has been there for him through thick and thin, and he is blessed to have her."

"Thick and thin, my ass. You shouldn't put that much trust in her, and neither should he."

"Why? Because you know something that we don't? I guess you're going to announce that you've been screwing her too."

There was silence. I could tell that my tone annoyed Cedric, but I didn't care. I couldn't help it.

He finally spoke. "She's not my type, and I'm surprised that he's stuck with her this long. Her head game must be fierce."

That about did it for me. I didn't have anything else to say other than "I'll see you later."

After that, I moseyed on by the liquor cabinet, thinking hard about making a drink. I needed a little something to calm me before Cedric got here, but after I began to pour myself a drink, I stopped. I poured the liquid down the drain, then rinsed the glass. To keep myself busy, I started to clean up. I vacuumed the floors, washed a few dishes, and then cleaned Jacoby's bathroom. I noticed two condoms in his trash can, and I was kind of pissed that he and Adrianne had been having sex in his room. I wasn't sure if I was going to call him out on it or not, especially since tonight would wind up being hectic for all of us.

When Jacoby came home, he kissed my cheek, then rushed to get something to eat in the kitchen. As he sat at the kitchen table, eating two hot dogs and some chips, I sat with him.

"Are you nervous about this evening? Cedric said he would be here around six or seven."

Jacoby shrugged. "I'm a little nervous, but I'm ready to get this over with. Whatever he decides to do is up to him. And whatever my punishment may be, I'll accept it."

"There will be no punishment. You've already suffered enough."

"Unfortunately, Mom, that won't be for you to decide."

Hearing him say that made my stomach hurt. Now I needed that drink even more than I had needed it earlier. Jacoby seemed much calmer than I was, and when the doorbell rang almost an hour later, he still seemed calm. I was flustered. I almost tripped on a rug as I made my way to the front door, and when I swung it open, it was not Cedric. Instead, it was Justin. I hadn't seen him since we had sex at the hotel, and we had talked on only one occasion after that. For him to show up at my door was a total surprise. His timing couldn't be more off, but I didn't want to be rude.

"Normally," he said, "I don't just pop up like this, but I was in your neighborhood. Just thought I'd stop by to say hello and find out what you were doing this weekend. There's a jazz concert at the park. I remember you telling me how much you like jazz. We don't have to go as a couple or anything like that, but it would be nice to hang out with you again."

I didn't mind hanging out with Justin, but I had to let him know that this thing between us wasn't going anywhere. I told him just that as I invited him inside and asked him to have a seat in the living room. I closed the French doors just so Jacoby wouldn't hear our conversation.

"I suspected that it wasn't that serious for you," he said, raking his hair back with his fingers. "And that's fine with me. You're fresh off of a divorce, and I get that the last thing you want to do is jump into another relationship."

"I'm glad you understand. Feel free to call me on Friday. If I'm not doing anything, I would love to meet you at the park. It sounds like fun, and jazz music is my favorite."

Justin started to tell me about some of the artists he loved. I enjoyed his company, but as it was nearing seven o'clock, I tried to rush him out the door before Cedric got there. My attempt, however, was too late. Cedric knocked on the door, and when Jacoby opened it, he came inside. I could see him from where I was sitting, and he could see me. The person he couldn't see was Justin, until he came closer to the French doors and opened them. His eyes shifted to Justin, who had stood right along with me.

"Justin, this is my ex-husband, Cedric. Cedric, this is a friend of mine," I said.

Justin politely extended his hand, but all Cedric did was look at it. "Friend of yours?" he said. "Since when did you start having friends that I don't know about?"

I was taken aback by his tone and his comment. And his poor treatment of Justin really disturbed me. "I'm not required to tell you about any of my friends. How dare you come in here like you live here or something?"

He pointed his finger right at the tip of my nose. "Don't disrespect me. I may not live here, but you'd better believe that it was my fucking money that bought everything up in here. I paid for that sofa he's been sitting his ass on, and I got a problem with you inviting muthafuckas up in here who don't help to pay the bills."

To say I was in shock would be putting it mildly. I didn't know where all of this was coming from. He needed to correct himself quickly or else. Justin just stood there, as if he didn't know what to say or do. He appeared even more shocked than I was.

"You need to apologize to my guest. If you don't, you need to leave and try this again at another time. I don't understand how you think you pay all the bills around here, and just in case you don't know, my bank account has my name on it, not yours."

"Excuse me," Justin said. "I—I think it'll be best if I just go. I didn't mean to cause any trouble, and, Kayla, I will see you at the park this weekend."

"Yeah, it is best that you go," Cedric said. "And don't you ever bring yo' ass back here again."

This was too much to swallow. I stopped Justin from exiting, then stood face-to-face with Cedric. "He's staying right here. And you're the one who needs to go. I don't know what has gotten into you, Cedric, but you will not come over here and try to run anything."

Jacoby stood by the door, trying to calm the situation, which was minutes from boiling over. "Dad, why don't you just go? I'll call you tomorrow, and we'll talk then."

"I'm not going no damn where!" Cedric yelled. "This sucker got one minute to get the fuck out of here, or else he's going to find my foot in his ass."

"And you're going to find mine in yours," I fired back. "Stop this madness and get out! Now, Cedric, before I call the police on you."

Justin didn't want any part of this. He took a few steps forward to leave, and I got the shock of my life when Cedric lifted his foot and punted Justin in his ass. I gasped as Justin turned around and swung at Cedric. He ducked, and before I knew it, the two of them were going at it. This was unbelievable to me. I yelled for them to stop, but my screams fell on deaf ears. Cedric held on tight to Justin's neck as he was bent over, and then he rammed Justin's head into my French doors. Glass shattered, and one of the doors fell off its hinges.

Justin kept punching Cedric in his legs to weaken him, but he was no match for Cedric. He lifted Justin up high, then slammed him down in the foyer. As Cedric punched him in the face, I saw blood splatter everywhere. Jacoby and I tried to pull Cedric off Justin, but Cedric was in a rage. He shoved me back so hard that I fell and almost bumped my head on the table. Justin attempted to get away from him, and that was when Cedric and Jacoby started to argue.

"Stop it, Dad! Now!"

"Back the fuck up, Jacoby. You don't want none of this, trust me!"

Cedric refused to let Justin get out the door. He punched him in his chest, then lit up his stomach with several hard blows. As Justin dropped to one knee, Cedric punched him so hard in the face that I thought I heard something crack. I cried hard as I jumped on his back to stop him. That was when I saw Jacoby lift his shirt and remove a gun from the inside of his jeans.

"Push her again, and I'll shoot." Jacoby held the gun near Cedric's temple. "Now, do like she said, and get the hell out of here. You ain't got no business coming here and doing all of this. In case you didn't get the memo, the damn marriage is over!"

There Jacoby was, trying to defend me again. I removed myself from Cedric's back, and he stood up straight with caution and ease.

"Put it away, Jacoby," I said, looking at Justin, who seemed to be in a lot of pain as he swayed back and forth on the floor. "Put the gun away. This is ridiculous, and I'm calling the police."

"Call them," Cedric said, with calm in his voice. "I can't wait for them to get here. Ain't no telling who will go to jail, though, and it very well may not be only me."

His eyes shifted to Jacoby. The look in Cedric's eyes told me that he knew what Jacoby had done. Cedric reached for the gun, demanding that Jacoby give it to him. "You shouldn't be carrying anything around like that. Guns are dangerous, and people can get hurt by them. Trust me, I know. I have the scars to prove it, and you wouldn't want to be put in a position where you have proof too."

I rushed up to Jacoby and snatched the gun from his hand. It was better if it was in my hands than in his or Cedric's.

"Go, Cedric. Please go," I pleaded. "You've done enough tonight. You should be ashamed of yourself for carrying on like this in front of your son."

"Trust me, I'm not. I'm no more ashamed than you should be for fucking this young punk and allowing him to come to a place where I pay the bills at. You can do better than this, Kayla, and before you bring any motherfucker up in here again, in front of my son, you need to seek my approval. If not, I will kick ass again, just like I did his."

Before he walked out the door, Cedric lifted his foot and kicked Justin in his face. I was crushed, and even though I wanted to call the police, I couldn't. I rushed over to Justin to comfort him.

"Jacoby, go get me a wet towel and some ice. Hurry."

I helped Justin up off the floor and held him up as I he limped over to the sofa.

"Hey," he strained to say while holding his side, "it's not as bad as it looks."

To me, it looked pretty bad. His face was bruised. Right eye was almost shut, and blood ran from his nose. I saw bruises on his neck, and I could only imagine what the rest of his body looked like.

"If you want, I can drive you to the hospital and take you to the police station so you can press charges against him. I am so sorry about this, and I feel horrible that this has happened to you."

Jacoby came into the room with two wet towels and a bucket of ice. He also offered to take Justin to the hospital.

"No," Justin said while squeezing his head with his fingertips. "I'm okay. I just need to get cleaned up. That's all."

I did my best to clear the blood from his face. I also put ice on it. When I helped him remove his shirt, I saw that his chest and his side were bruised.

"I can't let you sit there like this. Let me take you to the hospital. Please."

He refused. Said he didn't want to go, but he did go to my bathroom to clean himself up better than I had. While looking in the mirror, he touched his swollen face.

"Damn. He's good," Justin said, then released a chuckle. "He banged me up pretty bad, didn't he?"

"I don't see how you can find humor in all of this. I can't, Justin, and I want you to press charges against him."

Justin ignored my request. I didn't know if he had warrants out or not, but he refused to go to the police station. He also refused once more to go to the hospital, and it was almost two hours later when he decided to leave and go home.

"Thanks for taking care of me," he said. "I still hope to see you on Saturday, but if not, I won't be mad at you."

I refused to put him in a situation like this again. Lord knows, I was hurt, and yet I had to admit that this was on me.

"I may or may not see you at the park, but please go home and take care of yourself. If you change your mind about going to the hospital, call me. I'll take you, and I will do anything else that you need me to do."

Justin reached out and gave me a hug. He squeezed me tight, then gave me a kiss on the cheek. I took that as a sign that I would never see him again.

After he left, I went to Jacoby's room to talk to him. He was on the phone and acted as if he didn't want to be interrupted.

"Not now, Mama. Please. I just need to chill."

"Where in the hell did you get that gun? I don't like you carrying that thing around, and I had no idea that you had it."

"I got it to protect myself."

"Protect yourself from who?"

"From whoever."

"Well, you won't have it to protect yourself from whomever it is that you're protecting yourself from. I have it now, and you won't be getting it back."

"Fine. Now, is there anything else you'd like to get off your chest?"

"Plenty of stuff, but I'm not going there with you tonight."

I left his room, upset with him for having the gun, furious with Cedric for clowning as he had tonight, and livid with Evelyn for telling Cedric my secret. I was anxious to speak to Cedric again, but I intended to wait a few more days to let things cool down. I grabbed a bottle of Hennessy Black and took it to my bedroom with me so I, too, could chill.

10

Evelyn

I was starting to get bored with shopping. Over the past several weeks, I had spent at least two hundred thousand dollars on material bullshit that didn't make me feel better. The car I had purchased was included, and after driving my new Mercedes for one week, it felt like any other car to me.

The only thing I was excited about was moving . . . and the time I'd spent with Charles. I couldn't stop thinking about that man. I couldn't remember the last time I had felt this attached to someone. With Cedric, it was all about the money. I put up with that fool because I wanted his money, and I was trying to secure a future with a man who had it. Charles being wealthy was a plus, but it didn't matter to me either way. There was something about him that moved me big-time.

That was too bad for me, because I wasn't supposed to reach out to him again. I had promised him, as well as myself, that all I needed was one day. One day to do exactly what we'd done, but I was to the point where I wanted more. I hadn't heard from him, but that didn't surprise me. He didn't have my number to reach me, but I was 100 percent sure that if he wanted to get in touch, he would.

For now, I went into chill mode and turned my thoughts to moving. First of all, I wanted a bigger place, but more than anything, I wanted to get the hell away from Cedric. My apartment had too many bad memories. Memories of Cedric, of Bryson, and of some of the other useless men I'd brought there from time to time. I needed a fresh start, and the new town house I had found was in a peaceful neighborhood, and only twenty minutes away from my BFF Kayla.

I was a little perturbed because I hadn't heard from her. I had called to check on her several times, but she hadn't replied. When I'd reached out to Trina, she hadn't called me back, either. I wondered what was up with them, especially Kayla and her little drinking problem. A huge part of me felt terrible for her. My original plan had been to tell Cedric everything, but I just couldn't do it. I didn't want to keep hurting Kayla and Jacoby, and I had realized that they had been hurt enough not only by me, but by Cedric, as well. Together, we had caused enough damage.

He just couldn't stop, and he got carried away. He had started talking slick and taking advantage of me again. Treating me like shit and putting his hands on me wasn't the route to go. I had an idea about how I was going to deal with him, but the one thing that I wasn't going to do was tell him anything about Jacoby trying to kill him. The truth was, something inside of me felt as if he already knew. In my heart, I believed that Cedric had put this little scheme together to cause more chaos between me and my BFF's. He was too much of a wise man to sit back and wait on me for information. That just didn't seem right, and whenever I saw him again, I intended to share my thoughts.

The movers were at my place, boxing up everything for me. I was so ready to get out of here, and I had already taken some of my things over to the new place. I called Trina and Evelyn to see if they wanted to come see my new town house, but the only person I got in touch with was Trina.

"Of course I want to see it, but you and I have some things that we need to discuss. If I come over there, will I be in the way?"

"No. The movers are almost done, and the majority of my things won't be moved out of here until tomorrow. Come on over. I'll be here."

Trina told me she was on her way. While waiting for her to come, I went into my bedroom and started to put some of my shoes in a box.

"I'll get those," one of the movers said. "I'm just working on your other closet right now."

"That's fine. You work on that one, and I'll work on this one. I don't mind helping."

He got back to work, and so did I. But the whole time I packed, I couldn't shake my thoughts of Charles. It still *felt* like his dick was inside me, only because every time I thought about it, there was a throb that came from deep within. I wanted so badly not to think about him, but something strange was happening to me. Something that I knew I wasn't ready for. Something that felt kind of scary.

I finished up in the closet, then thanked the movers who had been there to help me.

"We'll be back around eight in the morning," one of them said. "Is that too early for you?"

"No, that's perfect. How long do you think it will take?"

"Probably about three or four hours, drive time included. But keep in mind that if you're not happy with our services, you don't have to pay."

"So far, so good. I'll see you guys in the morning. And thanks again."

As they were leaving, Trina was on her way in. She looked really cute in her soft pink sweats and a crop top that showed her tight abs. Out of all of us, she was the one who kept herself real fit. She had muscles, but not the ones that made a woman look manly. Her short, layered hair swerved to one side, and her bangs rested on her forehead. As she passed by me, I smacked her big ass, which looked to be growing.

"No wonder Keith is in love," I said playfully. "And it looks to me like he's been working that thing out."

"All day, every day," she said, then made her way into the living room and took a seat on the sofa. "And while he's been working me out, I hope like hell you aren't still working Cedric out."

Her comment stunned me. I had thought that my secret was safe with Cedric. Did Trina know something that I didn't?

I sat down on the sofa. "What do you mean by that?"

"What I mean is, you have some explaining to do. Kayla stopped by your place the other night and saw Cedric's car over here. If you expect me or her to believe that y'all were in here building blocks, then I'll have to ask you to come again."

I wanted to lie to Trina, but I decided to come clean. I told her about him visiting me at the hospital, and about him asking me to give him information about Kayla and Jacoby. I also admitted to having sex with him again.

"After we left Bryson's parents' house, I went there with him again. I also had sex with him a few more times after that, but that's because he keeps coming over here and making demands. He is out of control, and I fear that he may do something to me or Kayla."

Trina's lips were pursed the whole time I spoke. "You don't expect me to believe you, do you? I mean, come on, Evelyn. Cedric can't make you do anything that you don't want to do. And why would you agree to tell him anything about Jacoby and Kayla? So what you're telling me is you were being fake with her. You were around only to pump information from her?"

"No. I've been hanging out with y'all because we're friends, and that's what friends do. At first I was on the fence, only because I felt as if I owed Cedric. Then, after seeing Kayla break down like that the other day, I just couldn't do it. I haven't told Cedric one single thing, even though I know what Jacoby did."

"Please forgive me, but I'm having a hard time believing you. Yet again, Kayla is so upset with you, and I can't say that I blame her. You need to stop this, Evelyn. I don't know what you're trying to gain by your constant betrayals, but when will enough be enough?"

Trina was starting to upset me. I didn't know what else to say to her, especially since I was speaking the truth.

"I don't know how long I'm going to have to pay for my mistakes. Yes, I've done some dirty things, and as you can see, I'm trying to make up for those things. I have no reason to sit here and lie to you. It was difficult for me to admit that I've still been screwing Cedric, but I told you that because I want to be clear about how I feel about him. I do not love him, I have never loved him, and the only reason I messed around with him was that I needed his money. I know that sounds crazy, but it's the truth."

"And you're still messing around with him because you need his money, right? How could that be the case when you're supposed to be over here, sitting pretty with the money Mr. and Mrs. Washington gave you? All I'm saying is, something doesn't add up."

I just shook my head. I swore I needed some new friends. What was so difficult to understand about this?

"It may not add up to you, but it adds up to me. I just said that the only reason I started fucking with Cedric again was that he helped me out of a situation that I had no way out of. You know darn well that I didn't have a dime to defend myself in court. Bryson's parents were about to eat me alive, until Cedric reached out to them.

He turned that whole situation around, and I had to promise him something in return."

Trina sat silent. She rolled her eyes at me a few times and then released a deep breath. "Instead of telling me all of this, why don't you call Kayla? You really need to have this conversation with her, not me."

"I'm having this conversation with you because you said you wanted to talk. I don't mind telling Kayla what I just told you, but I assure you that I'll get the same response. She will not listen to me, and she is set on me being a horrible person who can't be redeemed."

Trina didn't say anything, but she knew I had spoken the truth. And at this point, I just didn't care anymore. I was sure Trina would relay everything I'd said to her to Kayla. If she wanted to talk further about it, I was sure she would reach out to me.

"I did say that I wanted to talk," Trina finally said. "And if that's going to be your explanation for all of this, then so be it. On another note, when can I see your new town house?"

"We can go over there now. Do you have time?"

Trina said she did, so we got in her car and left. On the drive there, she was real quiet. I asked what was on her mind. That was when she mentioned her trip to New York tomorrow.

"So you decided to go, huh?" I said.

"Yep. I need to stabilize my career, and I'm due to meet with some important people on Friday."

"What kind of important people?"

"I just told you. People who may help me stabilize my career."

"So you have to go all the way to New York to find people who can help you stabilize your career? That makes no sense to me, and like you told me earlier, I think you may need to come again."

Trina swallowed and continued to speak to me with an attitude. She did that often when she felt guilty about something. "If you don't mind, I don't want to talk about my trip. I have a lot of things on my mind right now, and talking about it isn't going to help much."

"Okay. I won't push like you push me when I don't want to talk. But I do have to ask how Keith feels about your trip."

"He thinks I'm going on a three-day vacation with you and Kayla. So, whatever you do, please don't call me at home, don't call my cell, and do not call him."

Trina was playing with fire. And she had the audacity to try to make me feel bad about my situation with Cedric. He wasn't the one she should be concerned about. If she wanted to be mad at me, she should be mad at me about having sex with the one who could be her possible father-in-law. Since she didn't know about us yet, I guessed she couldn't be mad.

"I won't call Keith, and as a matter of fact, I have no reason to call him. While I don't approve of what you're doing, I'm not going to sit here and judge you like you judge me. Especially when I . . ." I paused, then changed my mind. "Never mind. Forget it. Make a right at the light, and at the first street, make a left."

"Forget what?" Trina said, following my directions. "What were you going to say?"

"Nothing. Now, drive all the way to the end of the street, and my town house is on the left."

Trina drove farther down the street, then parked her car. She looked at the town houses, then nodded. "These are nice. Must have cost you a fortune. But what were you about to say?"

"I said never mind."

"And I said tell me. I hate when you do that, Evelyn. You need to quit it."

"I'm hesitant to tell you because the last time I told you a secret, it got back to Bryson, and he wound up beating my ass. You do remember that, don't you, my dear friend?"

Trina looked down; then she started fumbling with her nails. "I'm sorry about that, but I had no idea Bryson was that kind of man. And even though you told me he would hurt you, I didn't think he would go that far."

"You mean, you didn't believe me. Just like you don't believe what I just told you about me and Cedric."

"Let's not go there again, but go ahead and tell me what you were about to say. I won't say anything to anybody, especially not Kayla."

"Kayla's not the one I'm worried about. I'm worried about you telling Keith."

"I don't like to keep things from him, but you already know that I have been keeping some secrets. Whatever your secret is, if you don't want him to know, then I won't say anything."

I paused for a few seconds, then let it out. "Even if it's about his father?"

A tiny frown appeared on Trina's face. "His father? Is there something he should know about his father? If so, Evelyn, you'd better tell me. I don't want Keith to get hurt again, like he did when you broke it down about Bryson."

"I wouldn't want Keith to get hurt again, either, so my lips are sealed."

Trina wasn't having it. She wouldn't get out of the car unless I elaborated more. "You are so wrong, Evelyn. Did you see him with someone? And please don't tell me that you saw him with a man too."

"No, trust me when I say it was nothing like that. He is, indeed, one hundred percent all man. I can assure you of that."

Trina looked as if she had stopped breathing. Her mouth dropped open, and she sat up straight in her seat.

"Evelyn, please don't tell me what I think you're trying to tell me. Are you fucking Keith's father?"

I looked straight ahead, then zipped my lips. "I have nothing to say."

"Like hell!" Trina shouted. "Tell me now. Then again, no. Don't tell me. I don't want to know. 'Cause if you did, I would definitely have to tell Keith. But as far as I'm concerned, this conversation didn't happen. I don't want to know anything, and please take me inside to see your new place."

"I will. After I tell you how freaking big his dick is. Girl, that thing is about this damn long, and he beat the shit out of me with it." I tried to show Trina the measurements with my hands, but she turned her head and covered her ears.

"Nope," she said. "I didn't hear a word you said. All I heard you say was, 'The weather sure is nice outside.'"

I laughed, then pulled her hands away from her ears. "Huge, girl, and your dear friend is hooked! It only happened one time, but I can't stop thinking about him. Are things that serious between him and his wife? Do you know if the marriage is solid or not?"

Trina started to hum. She tapped her feet on the floor of the car, then covered her ears once again. That was when I opened the car door.

"Fine then. Let's go inside," I said.

I got out of the car, and so did Trina. As we made our way to my front door, she walked behind me.

"You know what?" she said. "I think there is a motive behind everything you do. You knew that if you told me about you and Mr. Washington, I would tell Keith. And Keith would tell his mother and confront his father. A whole lot of shit would get stirred up, and then Mr. Washington may come running to you. That's what you want to happen, but just so you know, I'm not telling

Keith one word. The holes you dig keep on getting deeper. I promise you that he is not the kind of man you want to fuck with."

I didn't respond, but Trina knew me all too well. I did have a motive for telling her, and it was just that. While she said she wouldn't tell Keith, in my heart, I felt that she would.

The next day I was all moved into my new town house. It was sweet. Had a spacious loft area, three bedrooms, two and a half bathrooms, and a luxury kitchen. I had so much room, and I intended to use one of the bedrooms as an office. In order to keep myself busy, I had to start a business or invest in one. Whenever I was ready, I had the place to do it.

Most of my furniture had been delivered, and this go-around I had gone the classic contemporary route. The walls were a light gray, and most of my furnishings were soft yellow and silky white. I was totally impressed by some of the things I had picked out. The interior designer I had hired to hook up everything for me had said she couldn't make it over until the weekend. I had wanted to ask Trina to help me, but I didn't like her taste. She liked loud colors—colors that could blind a person when they came into a room. I hoped that she wouldn't take offense at me for not asking her and hiring someone else.

After the sun went down, I sat on my new plush sofa and thought about calling her. Then I remembered what she had told me about going to New York. I was worried about that little situation, but I figured that Trina and Keith would someway or somehow work it all out.

I got up from the sofa to go turn on some music. Kayla wasn't the only one who could afford to have an intercom that played music throughout the home. I was now balling too, and it certainly felt good. So good that I got me a cigarette, poured a drink, and then went outside on my balcony. I took a few puffs from the cig, then whistled smoke into the air. Thoughts of Charles quickly invaded my mind. I visualized myself on that bed, getting the royal treatment again. The way he held my waist from behind and gave me inch by inch had felt spectacular. I had gone crazy and had never leaked that much in my life. My thoughts of him got so deep that I backed up to the wrought-iron lounge chair and let my silk robe fall to the side. I smashed the cigarette in an ashtray, then cocked my legs open. Hot and more than bothered, I slipped two of my fingers inside my pussy. I closed my eyes while sliding my fingers in and out of me. They felt nothing like Charles, and a few minutes in, I gave up.

I went inside, snatched up my cell phone, then punched in his number. On the second ring, he answered. His masculine voice uttering a simple word like "hello" made my pussy dance.

"Charles, this is Evelyn," I said in a soft tone.

There was a pause. Then he responded, "What do you want?"

"You. I want you. I need to see you again."

The only thing I heard was the call drop. I wasn't sure if he had done it intentionally or not, but when I called back, his phone went to voice mail. I tried three times, and after that, my number was blocked. I was completely taken aback. I guessed he meant what he'd said about going there only once, and I was highly upset about it. I didn't know what to do about his ill treatment, but surely I'd think of something.

11

Trina

The big day had finally arrived. I had stayed up late last night, packing and making love to Keith, and afterward, I hadn't gotten much sleep, maybe an hour or two. When I woke up, I found him in the kitchen, cooking breakfast. He was in his black Calvin Klein briefs that melted on his perfect ass. His colorful tats were on display, and his smooth chocolate skin made me want to have him again for breakfast. When he turned around, my eyes dropped to his mountain of love, which appeared to be hard.

"What are you thinking about, other than my breakfast?" I teased.

"I was thinking about how bad you put it on me last night." He laughed, then slid my pancakes on a plate. "I couldn't let you leave here hungry."

"Thank you," I said, walking up to him to give him a kiss. "But I only have time to eat one. I'm running behind, and I really need to get out of here. Kayla and Evelyn are already on their way to the airport."

"Do you need me to drop you off?"

"No. I'm going to drive and leave my car in the parking lot. When I return, I don't want to wait for you to pick me up."

"Okay. We'll hurry up and eat. Give me some suga and go."

I wished I had time to give him more than that, but I didn't. I ate the pancake and a few pieces of bacon. Guzzled down some orange juice, then gathered my luggage, which was already at the door.

"Let me help you with that," Keith said as I put the straps from one of the bags on my shoulder.

"I have only two bags. I got it, but thanks."

I puckered my lips for a kiss, Keith obliged, and that kiss instantly turned intense. Keith was the one who backed away from it.

"Don't start nothing you can't finish," he said. "Have fun, and don't forget to call me when you get to Vegas."

I assured him that I would call. I surely intended too, and the second I got on the plane, regret and guilt washed over me. I wasn't sure how this trip was going to pan out. For one thing, I knew it wasn't all about business.

I was in New York in no time at all. Was glad I didn't have any layovers and the plane was on time. I had asked Sasha to meet me at LaGuardia, and, sure enough, while as I was waiting for my luggage, she appeared.

My heart skipped a beat when I saw her, but I tried to play down my enthusiasm. Her beauty couldn't be denied. I loved her Afrocentric style. And she was one sexy woman. Part of her hair was now braided in a knot, with some of the braids falling far down her back. She wore a loud yellow tank and a colorful skirt. Her heels had ribbons on them that tied around her ankles. A red, yellow, green, and black necklace gathered around her neck, and her makeup was flawless, like the paint on a great work of art.

The first thing she did was walk up and give me a hug. Her breasts pressed against mine, and her sweet perfume drew me right in.

"No words can express how delighted I am to see you," she said. "Thank you so much for coming."

"No, thank you for inviting me. I'm waiting on my luggage. It should be here in a minute or two."

We waited for almost fifteen minutes for my luggage to come. Afterward, we walked together to her car, and within thirty minutes, we were at my hotel.

"You don't have to stay here, you know," she said. "The last thing I want you to do is waste money."

"Well, hopefully, I'll be in a position to get some of that money back. I'm excited about the meeting on Friday. Did you get those pictures I shipped to you?" I had shipped three of my paintings to Sasha so she could share them with the individuals I planned to meet tomorrow.

She confirmed that she had gotten them. "They arrived late yesterday, so I haven't had time to show them to anyone. But they are breathtaking. You certainly have talent, and your pictures need to be on display in museums."

I'd never gotten compliments like that about my work. Not even from Keith. And even though I was good, I didn't think I was that good. Then again, yes, I was.

Sasha helped me unpack my things, and then we headed to the sandwich shop in the lobby so I could get something to eat. Sasha couldn't join me, so we parted ways outside the sandwich shop.

"Don't eat that much," she said. "I'm taking you to dinner later, and then we're going out to have some fun, before we take care of business. Try to get some rest, and I'll pick you up around seven or eight tonight."

She gave me another hug before prancing away. I felt good about being here, and when I returned to the room after having a sandwich, I quickly called Keith to let him know I had arrived.

"We're here," I said, lying my ass off. "It's steaming hot, but we're going to go walk the Strip and see what's up."

"Try to stay cool and drink plenty of water. How was your flight?"

"A little bumpy, but we made it. Evelyn and Trina are already arguing, but you know how they are."

"Yes, I do. Don't get in the middle, and if they start fighting, you need to come home. I'm missing you already."

"Yeah, me too. What are your plans for today?"

"I'm going to hang out with Chris and Shawn at the pool hall tonight. We also have plans to go to a strip club," he said, laughing.

"Strip club, my ass. You'd better not be spending your time at a strip club, especially when you have all of this."

"I agree. I was only kidding, and I'm well aware of what I have. Love you, baby, and I'll see you soon."

"Yes, you will."

I hung up, then fell back on the bed. I drifted off as I thought about our relationship, and then my thoughts shifted to Evelyn and Keith's father. Since yesterday I'd been pondering the question of whether I should tell Keith, but that would give him another reason to hate Evelyn even more. I also felt as if it was none of my business, but then again, Keith was my business. The last time I had thought that way was when I discovered that Evelyn was having sex with Cedric behind Kayla's back. Keeping that from her had been the wrong thing to do. I just wasn't sure if spilling the beans was the right thing to do this time, but I did know that keeping all these secrets wasn't good for anyone.

I fell asleep while in thought, and when I woke up, it was already several minutes after six. I quickly got up to shower, and since Sasha said we would be going out tonight, I decided to put on a mustard-yellow pantsuit I'd brought. The jacket buttoned at my waist, and the pants fit like leggings. Even though I didn't like to wear heels, I rocked them, anyway. I swooped my layered hair to the side, spiked the front a little, then sprayed a dash of perfume between my breasts, which were visible due to the low-cut jacket. The only thing I had underneath it was my bra, which you could barely notice was there.

Sasha had told me to meet her in the lobby. By the time I had gotten all dolled up, she was already there. She still had on the skirt and the accessories from earlier, but instead of the tank, she now had on a jacket. From a short distance, I could see the lust in her eyes as she scanned me from head to toe. A wide smile appeared on her face, and a compliment followed.

"You are so beautiful," she said. "Anybody ever tell you that you look like Kelly Roland?"

"Trust me, I hear it all the time." I laughed.

I made my way to her car with her. The club we went to was less than five miles away, and when we got inside, it was jam-packed. Sasha had reserved a table for us. We sat close to a stage, but nothing was happening there yet.

"What's going on here tonight?" I asked, then took a seat.

"You'll see. It's a surprise."

A waiter came over to the table to ask what we wanted to drink. I wasn't a heavy drinker, so I ordered a wine cooler. Sasha ordered a Long Island Iced Tea.

"I'll be right back," the waiter said. "We also serve food. Would you ladies like anything else?"

"Yes," Sasha said. "I want my friend to try the Strawberry Shrimp. The chicken is good too, so I'll order chicken also."

The waiter left to place our order, and after he came back with our drinks, we delved into a conversation about Sasha and her girlfriend. Things seemed pretty rough, but when we turned the page to Keith and me, I had nothing but nice things to say. Jealousy was trapped in Sasha's eyes, and it made me kind of skeptical about her, because I had seen a similar look in Lexi's eyes whenever I spoke of Keith. Regardless, I told the truth and let her know that everything was good with us.

"He's the best," I said. "I have no complaints about my man whatsoever, except that he doesn't always put the toilet seat down. I can certainly live with that."

I laughed, but she didn't. The expression on her face was serious.

"Do you *want* to live with that? What I mean is, are you happy? Are you fully committed to him, and if so, why do I sense that you want to pursue something with me?"

I sipped from my drink, then sat the glass on the table. "I am happy, but sometimes, I just want to see what else is out there. I don't think that I've allowed myself an opportunity to figure out why I still find myself attracted to some women."

"It's because you fit the definition of *bisexual*. It's that simple, and your only problem is that you are trying to fight it. Embrace it and learn to accept it."

"Yeah, I guess. Been fighting it for too long, but I seriously thought that falling in love would make me swing one way or the other. I feel as if I'm in the middle."

"That's because you are. Maybe one day you won't be. But one thing I'm certain of is this. If you're still in the middle, as you say, then Keith isn't the one for you."

I disagreed, but I didn't say it. I didn't want to spend the evening defending my relationship with Keith, so I moved on to our plans for tomorrow. "What time are we supposed to meet tomorrow?" I asked.

"They'll be at my place around noon. I can't pick you up, because I need to set up everything. I have some other displays that I want to show them, and I didn't have time to lay everything out today."

"Just be sure to give me your address again. I'll take a cab."

Sasha wrote her address on a napkin. We conversed some more and ordered a few more drinks to wash down our food. Rap music thumped in the background, and when a famous rapper came through the door, many people rushed over to get his autograph, as well as his attention. A few minutes later the black curtains on the stage opened, and out came two female strippers with nothing on but thongs. With us sitting front and center, I saw everything. One of the strippers blew Sasha a kiss, and she waved at her.

"That's Black Pearl," Sasha said to me. "A good friend of mine. I've known her for years."

I felt uncomfortable sitting up close, and on a for-real tip, this wasn't my cup of tea. I watched males and females have their way with the strippers, making money rain on them. There was no question that the ladies had it going on. My eyes were glued to them, and I even had some nasty thoughts swarming in my head. Still, I couldn't get with this, especially when Black Pearl came over to us and Sasha started licking her nipples. I stood and told Sasha I was ready to go.

"What's wrong?" she said, looking shocked that I wanted to leave. "I brought you here to have some fun. Why is this setting bothering you?"

"It just does."

I walked away from the table, and after Sasha said something to Black Pearl, she followed me out the door. When we got to her car, she seemed slightly upset with me.

"Look, Trina. There was nothing wrong with us being in there. You just made me feel like shit. I had the whole night planned out for us, but now I guess you want to go back to the hotel, right?"

All kinds of thoughts were running through my head. It would be hypocritical of me to think that I could kick it at a strip club but Keith couldn't. I would have a fit if he did, and in addition to that, I was starting to feel bad about this whole thing.

When I was in thought, Sasha leaned in and pecked my lips. She waited for me to reciprocate, but I didn't. She softly kissed me again, and then she lifted her hand to my breast and squeezed it.

"If we go back to the hotel, can I join you? I don't want our night to end here, and it is my goal to make sure you have a wonderful time while you're here."

I licked my lips, just to see what hers tasted like. They were sweet and very inviting. Without responding, I leaned forward to kiss her. I touched her breasts, though I knew I shouldn't. Rubbed her soft legs, which I couldn't resist. Invited her to slip her fingers into me, and when I opened my legs, she reached inside my panties and did just that. The moment was extremely intense, and I had to take a deep breath and back away from it.

"Give me time to think about this, Sasha. I don't want to be rushed into this, okay?"

I was surprised that she didn't push. "Sure, Trina. Whenever you're ready, you know I'm here."

We climbed in the car, and she started it and then drove back to the hotel. We were there in no time. I thought she was going to go up to my room with me, but instead, she stayed in the car.

"I'll see you tomorrow. Have your sales pitch prepared, and get ready for what may be a new start for you," she said as I got out.

That made me feel better. Changed my whole demeanor. I was looking forward to tomorrow so I could hurry back home to my man. While I was feeling Sasha and her touch had aroused me, there was something about her that stopped me from going any further with her. I saw what Keith had seen, and I really didn't trust her.

The next day, I took a cab to the address Sasha had given me. The cabdriver parked in front of a brownstone that had an array of plants on the porch, and I paid the fare and climbed out. The small lawn in front was well manicured, and when I reached the porch and looked through the huge bay windows, I could see plenty of artwork covering the walls. I walked over to the tall door. I could see that it was open, but I still knocked. Nobody came to the door.

"Sasha," I called, then knocked again.

I could hear loud music coming from inside, so maybe she didn't know that I was at the door. I pushed the door open wider, and when I stepped inside, I saw my paintings, along with several others, propped up on easels. There were also a few folding chairs in front of a fireplace, and the smell of burning incense infused the air. Before going any farther, I called out to Sasha again but didn't get a reply. Then I heard something coming from another room. It sounded as if she was hurt. As if she was crying and needed help.

I rushed down a small, narrow hallway and then turned right. There was a room with an open door about ten steps in front of me. Didn't know what I was getting myself into and was nervous as hell. I had managed to grab a knife from the breakfast buffet I'd eaten at earlier, just in case. It was in my purse, and I held it close to me as I approached the open door. When I looked inside the room, I saw that Sasha was getting it on with Black Pearl, one of the strippers from last night. They both were moaning and groaning while caressing each other. Sasha stopped for a second to address me, with a smile on her face.

"What took you so long to get here?" she said while licking Black Pearl's neck with her curled tongue. "You're late, and we've been waiting on you."

I'd be lying if I said that seeing their near-perfect bodies in the bed, naked, didn't turn me on. I would not be telling the truth if I said I hadn't thought about being in a position like this with two other women. I couldn't deny that there was something in me that wanted to jump in that bed and have at it. But, deep down, I had to admit that there was something inside of me that outweighed all my thoughts. This just didn't feel right.

"I'm not late. You told me to be here at noon. Are we meeting some potential buyers or not?"

Sasha got off the bed in all her nakedness. She was as sexy as sexy could get. Lust was definitely in my eyes, and it made her smile when she noticed the attention I was giving her.

"They're going to be here, but not until later. We have plenty of time to explore each other, so why don't you take off your clothes and join us? I already told Black Pearl all about you, and from the look on her face, you can already see how delighted she is that you're here."

My eyes shifted to Black Pearl, who was kneeling on the bed, toying with her pussy. I was angry yet still slightly turned on. I attempted to be as nice as I could about the situation, since I didn't want to disrespect Sasha in her house.

"I didn't come here to explore sex with you or anyone else. I came to meet the individuals you said could possibly help with my career and would maybe purchase some of my paintings from me. If that's not going to happen, then I think I should leave."

Sasha stepped forward, leaving no breathing room between us. "I didn't say it wasn't going to happen. It just may not happen today, because, unfortunately, they called to cancel."

"Bullshit," I said, not holding back. "All you wanted to do was get me here to do this. Go ahead and admit it, Sasha. All you wanted was for me to come here so we could fuck."

With a smirk on her face, she reached out to touch my breast. I slapped her hand away, then moved backward.

"You do not have permission to touch me," I said. "Now, back the hell up and go back over there, where you're wanted."

Sasha turned to Black Pearl and pouted. "You hear that, baby? She doesn't want me. She's mad, and it looks as if I'm not good enough."

"If she doesn't want you, I do. Come on back over here so we can finish what we started. Let that bitch go back to wherever she came from."

Sasha sashayed back to the bed and wasted no time getting back to her lover. I swallowed the oversize lump in my throat. It wasn't until that moment that I realized just how stupid I was for coming here. I walked away, feeling awful. Didn't even bother to grab my paintings on my way out—just left empty-handed. Went back to the hotel, only to lie on the bed and listen to a voice mail from Keith.

"Hope you're having a good time, baby. But it's sad that a brotha can't get a phone call or nothing. Be sweet, and when you get back, I have something magnificent waiting for you. Until then, love you like the teddy bear I couldn't let go of until I was almost ten years old. I told you that story, but then again, I shouldn't have." He laughed, then ended the call.

Stupid me, I thought. *Stupid, fucking me*. I could have kicked myself in the ass for being here, so I hurriedly packed and got out of there. I had to pay a little extra to change my flight, but no ifs, ands, or buts about it, I was on my way back to St. Louis.

I sat at the airport for hours, waiting to get out of there. My phone kept ringing, and to no surprise, it was Sasha. My intention was to block her calls, but not until I told her how I was feeling.

"I don't know what you could possibly have to say to me after inviting me to come all the way to New York for this. You were wrong on so many different levels, and I do not want you to call me ever again."

"Trina, had I known you were so insecure, so stuck up, and were not willing to go there with me, I never would have asked you to come here. I guess I got the wrong impression of you from our conversations, and if so, I apologize. Now, why don't you come back to my place so we can talk? Black Pearl is gone, and it will be just you and me."

"Do I look that fucking stupid to you? Hell, no, I'm not coming back. You are out of your mind. And in reference to our conversations, you also understood that my main purpose for coming here was to meet with the people you kept talking about. I seriously thought you would be able to help me, but you know it was all a lie."

"It wasn't. I—I thought I'd be able to help you, but when I showed your paintings to a few people, they thought your stuff was basic. Basically, there was nothing really special about it, and the more I looked at it, the more I started to feel the same way too."

I hung up on that bitch, then blocked her number. Was she kidding me? Was she for real? I couldn't wait to get my ass back home, but unfortunately for me, as soon as I got back to St. Louis and was heading for my car, I looked up and saw Keith leaning against it. His arms were folded, and I surely didn't know that the look on his face could get that ugly. I smiled to play it off, but his face remained flat.

The only thing he said to me was, "How was your trip to New York?"

12

Kayla

I stood on the porch, with its five big columns and a wrought-iron, glass double door that offered a view of the interior of Cedric's new house. He'd sold the property where we used to live, and this was what he called downsizing. I had been here only once before, but I knew it was ten times better than the place in which we used to live. I guessed he had decided to go all out now that he was a bachelor.

I wasn't here to discuss any of that, though. I wanted to break it all down to him about Jacoby and also find out how much he knew. He obviously knew something. The way he had looked at Jacoby that last time said so. Then there was the issue of Justin. Cedric needed to do something . . . anything about that situation, and I was going to make sure that he knew where we stood. He couldn't come to my place anymore. I was done, and as far as I was concerned, I never had to deal with him again.

I rang the doorbell and could see Cedric's girlfriend, Joy, as she headed toward the door. There was a scowl on her face, and she had to be one of the saddest-looking women I had ever seen. I didn't understand why until she opened the door and I saw her blue-and-black eye, which looked real nasty. Seeing it almost took the breath out of me, and before I could say anything, she gave me an explanation.

"I know it looks bad, but I was in a car accident. I'm so thankful that I'm okay, but my car is completely totaled. Does Cedric know you were coming here today?"

"No, he doesn't, but is he here? Also, I'm sorry to hear about your accident, but I'm glad you are okay."

I had no problem with Joy, even though she had dated Cedric while we were married. I didn't find out about her until I broke into his house that day and saw her letters. The way I saw it, he was her problem now. Not mine.

After she let me inside and told me to have a seat in the living room, I saw Cedric coming down the hallway. He had on a blue silk robe and house shoes. A cigar dangled from his mouth, and as expected, there was no smile on his face. He evil eyed Joy, then cut his eyes at her. Without saying a word, she timidly walked away.

"You should have called before you came," he said.

"Yeah. Just like you do when you come to my place. I'm sure you were expecting my visit, so don't pretend that you weren't."

I was still standing, and he invited me to have a seat, but I didn't bother. I stood with my arms crossed, ready to let him have it.

"I need for you to tell me what you know," I said. "I do have some explaining to do, and I'm willing to do that, provided that you tell me why you're still having sex with Evelyn and how you found out about Jacoby."

He played clueless. "Evelyn who? Your best friend, Evelyn? No, I've had enough of that pussy, but I will say that she has shared some important things with me over the past few weeks. Things that shocked me and made me want to watch my back more than I'd been doing."

"Stop beating around the bush, Cedric. Important things like what?"

"I don't know, Kayla. Why in the fuck don't you tell me? I know you didn't come all the way over here to stand there and look pretty while talking shit."

"Keep you freaking compliments and save them for your hoes. I asked you a question, and I want some answers."

Cedric took a seat, chewed on the tip of the cigar, and then he laid it on an ashtray. He invited me to have a seat again, but I stayed right where I was at, all the while tapping my foot on the floor.

"Fine. Then stand your crazy ass there and be mad all you want to. If anybody should be mad, it should be me. I'm the one who's been lied to and plotted against. I'm the one who made sure you and Jacoby had everything y'all needed after our divorce, only to find out what the two of you had planned to do to me. I thought we could get along well as divorcés, and I am highly disappointed that I was wrong."

Lord knows, I was pissed. He had known and hadn't said a word.

"We were getting along well, until you started showing up at my place like you owned it. And what you did the other day was foul. You didn't have to do that young man like that. I am still trying to convince him to press charges against you."

"What a good way to change the subject and ignore what I just said. I don't give a damn about that fool coming to your place. He just happened to be in the wrong place at the wrong time. He caught me in one of my moods, and since I couldn't beat yo' ass like I wanted to, I settled for his."

"Beat my ass for what? I've done nothing to you. You're the one who has done everything to me. I haven't forgotten about all of it, Cedric. I may have forgiven you, but I have not forgotten how you treated me when I was married to you."

Cedric got up, then tied the belt on his robe tighter. He casually walked up to me and stood close. "Let's get real here," he said. "This has nothing to do with the way I treated you while we were married. The question is, do you really want me to stand here and explain to you what you did to me, or do you want me to pretend that I've been blind and can't see?"

"You have been blind if you—"

When I was in mid-sentence, Cedric lifted his fist and punched me clean in my right eye. He caught me so off guard that I stumbled back in my high heels and then fell hard on my ass. My eye felt as if it had been knocked from the socket, and my head throbbed. I placed my hand over my face and squeezed my watery eyes shut. Cedric stood over me, with his finger pointed near my face.

"I've waited a long time to do that. You have gotten away with too much shit, Kayla, and your biggest mistake was lying to me about Jacoby being my son. You want to talk about forgiveness? I will never forgive you for that. 'Cause you see . . . my son, my own flesh and blood, would never plot my demise. He would never want me dead, nor would he pay someone to kill me. You taught Jacoby to hate me. You wanted his plan to fall into place. That way you could have everything in life that I worked so hard to get, so that you could sit on your lazy ass, just like you're doing now, and do nothing. I know all about it, baby. Evelyn told me all about it, and it's too late for you to come over here and try to tell me anything. I don't want to hear one word from you, and you can tell Jacoby the same thing too."

With tears pouring down my face, I looked at Cedric with so much hate and anger inside of me. "Don't you dare talk to me about Jacoby! You are the one who destroyed him! You made him hate you by bringing all your tricks around him and by dogging his mother out. He felt like he had to do something to stop you. And I don't care what you've been told, but he didn't want to go through with it. He wanted to tell you, but I wouldn't let him!"

Cedric grabbed my neck and pushed my head back on the floor. I had never seen him like this. When we were married, not once had he put his hands on me. I didn't know who this man lying over me was. He had the look of a killer in his eyes. I tried to fight him and get him off of me, but he grabbed my arms and punched me in my face again. I felt blood trickling from my nose and flowing over my lips.

"That's your fucking problem now. You're always treating him like a baby, and you won't let him grow up and be a man. When a man wants to confront somebody about his wrongdoings, you need to move your ass out of the way and let him. But once again . . . ," he said, tightening his grip on my neck. He lifted my head, then slammed it hard on the floor. So hard that the back of my head stung. I didn't know if it was bleeding or not. "Once again, you felt it was best to keep secrets from me. You thought your way could save us all, and you were wrong, wrong, wrong!"

He banged my head three more times before letting me go. I rolled over. I was in so much pain. I seriously thought Cedric was going to kill me. I needed to get out of there fast.

He continued his tirade. "Then you bring your ass over here, talking shit about Evelyn. Hell, yeah, I'm still fucking her. Your pussy was never good enough, so a man gotta do what he must. You will never be better than her, and if it wasn't for her, I would still be left in the dark. I owe her my life, as well as a little more dick too."

I lifted my head and felt real dizzy. My eyes were blurry from crying, but I could see Joy a short distance away, biting her nails. She looked too afraid to say anything, and I now knew exactly where her black eye had come from. Cedric had lost his mind. Trying my best not to say anything else to him, I crawled my way to the door and reached for the knob. He grabbed both of my arms, then pulled them behind my back so hard that I thought they would break.

"You will not leave here without telling me you're sorry!" he yelled. "I want to hear you say it, and you damn well better mean it. Because if you don't, I am going to call the police right now and have them go to your place and arrest Jacoby. I have all kinds of proof about what he did, and I may even concoct some shit to have yo' ass arrested too."

My arms were hurting so bad that I had to say something. "So . . . sorry. I'm sooo sorry," I cried out, blood now dripping from my chin. "Now, please let me go, Cedric. You're hurting me!"

"Good! Now you know what it feels like to hurt. Tell me again, and this time, mean it! Leave all that other shit out of the mix!"

I swallowed hard, then lowered my head. "Sorry. Truly sorry for what I've done."

He let go of my arms, then pushed me away. He then opened the door and grabbed me by one of my arms. The next thing he did was toss me outside and slam the door behind me. My nose and my hands were bleeding, and so were my knees. I could see that my knees were bleeding through the holes in my jeans. I limped to my car, and if I could've called the police, I would have. I wanted to go home and get the gun I had taken from Jacoby, but if he saw me like this, I was sure that he would use the gun this time. I was a complete mess as I drove away, and I was mad as hell at Evelyn. She was the one who had told Cedric everything. I was going to make sure that she paid for running her big mouth.

Within an hour, I had stopped at a gas station to clean myself up and then had driven to Evelyn's apartment, only to discover that she didn't live there anymore. I had forgotten that Trina had told me in person that Evelyn had moved, and she had also told me so in her voice mail messages. But I didn't know where she had moved to. I called Trina to ask for Evelyn's address, but she was real short with me.

"I'll have to text it to you. Check your phone in five minutes," she said.

I could hear a male voice yelling in the background, but I didn't bother to ask if something was wrong. I just waited on her text message, and when I got it, I drove to Evelyn's new place, which wasn't too far from where I lived. It angered me that she was this close to me. And I hoped that this would be the last time I ever saw her face again.

Still banged up from what Cedric had done to me, I walked slowly to Evelyn's door, rubbing my sore arms. I knocked, and it wasn't long before she opened the door. As soon as her mouth opened, I slapped her across it. I then rushed inside and jumped on top of her. I pounded her head with my fists and yanked at her hair.

"Are you crazy!" she yelled out as she squirmed around on the floor. "Bitch, have you lost your mind!"

I didn't say a word. Just kept pounding away at her until I got tired. She tried to grab anything on me, but the only thing she could get ahold of was my shirt. She pulled on it so hard that she tore it off my body. After that, she bit my arm, then scratched the side of my face. That caused me to fall off of her. And when I did, she scurried into another room. I went after her and was met at her bedroom doorway by a nine millimeter. She aimed it at my head, trying to catch her breath. Her hands trembled as a tear rolled down her face.

"Put your hands on me again, and I will kill you, Kayla! What in the hell are you thinking?"

I wanted to go for the gun, but I already knew how unstable and jealous Evelyn was. She would blow my brains out, and somehow or someway she would make herself look like the victim. Afraid of that gun as I was, I still showed no fear as I told her how I felt about her betrayal.

"How dare you tell Cedric what I told you about Jacoby! You have caused my son great harm, all over a lousy dick that you just can't get enough of. I will never forgive you again, and this time you have really and truly gone too far. I don't even know how you sleep at night, Evelyn! Please tell me how in the hell you can live with yourself. You are the worst of the worst, and damn me for ever considering you my friend!"

Evelyn was breathing real hard, and her chest kept moving in and out. "I don't know what Cedric told you, but I did not tell him about Jacoby. He's playing you, Kayla. Playing you like a fool, and you're too blind to see it. I told Trina all about his plan, but I see that telling you will do no good. You are looking for someone to blame for all of this, and like always, that person is me."

"You're doggone right it is! And if you didn't tell Cedric about Jacoby, then who did? After all, you are the one who is still fucking him, aren't you? I guess you're going to lie about that too."

"I'm not going to lie about it, but I had my reasons. You—"

"Shut up!"

I wanted to break that heifer's neck, but when I moved forward, she squeezed the gun tighter and gave me a warning.

"Think before you make another move. As a matter of fact, turn around and get out of here. If you want to believe Cedric, fine. I have nothing else to say. What I know is, I'm not going to allow you to put your fucking hands on me again."

I was done with Evelyn and Cedric. I hadn't really wanted to come here, but I had had to. This was the last straw. Everybody had a breaking point. This was mine. I walked out her door, vowing never to let her back in my life again.

13

Evelyn

Wow. In all the years I had known Kayla, we had never fought like that. She was on a rampage. I was so confused by what Cedric had told her. I hadn't said one word to him, but there he was, lying on me again. I had figured he would do something like this, and when I called to chew him out, he laughed about it.

"You made your bed, so you need to lay in it," he said. "I told you that if you didn't get me the information I wanted, shit was going to start happening, didn't I? My only question to you is, did Kayla beat that ass, or did you beat hers? I would have loved to have been a fly on the wall to see who got the best of who."

"You're truly the devil, Cedric, and this is what I get for dancing with you. It would be so nice if Paula had killed you when she had the chance, and I should go straight to that jailhouse and slap her for not finishing the job."

"Awww, don't be so nasty, sugar pie. You weren't talking all that shit when I had my dick up, and just a few weeks ago, I was the best thing ever. I saved your life and made you a rich woman. According to you, you owed me big-time. Now, all of a sudden, my name is dirt. I'm not worth two cents, and you wish I was dead. That's no way to speak to a man who is on edge right now. And you'd better watch yourself, because I will give you a dose of what I gave your friend earlier."

I hung up on Cedric. He was cuckoo. I didn't know what he said or did to make Kayla believe him, but she should have known better. Why didn't she just come over here and ask me? I would have told her everything, even though I'd have figured that she wouldn't listen to me. I was concerned about Cedric winning this battle, so after I cleaned myself up and brushed my hair into a sleek ponytail, I called Trina to see if she had spoken to Kayla about our conversation.

"What is it?" she yelled when she picked up her phone. "I'm busy right now. I'll have to call you back!"

She hung up, and that was that. I guessed Kayla must've gotten to her before I did, and they were, once again, on the same team. I threw my hands in the air and then got back to what I was doing before Kayla came barging in here and interrupting me. I was in my office, doing research on the best way to invest my money. I knew that I couldn't keep spending it at the rate I was. If I didn't want it to get away from me, I had to start doing something that would make my money grow. I searched the Internet for a few hours or so. I also set up an appointment with a financial adviser, but I wasn't meeting with him until tomorrow. I then figured that Charles might be able to give me some good advice too, so I called his phone to see if my number was still blocked. After hearing his voice, I knew that I was back in business.

"Please do not hang up this phone," I said.

"You're hardheaded, Evelyn. I told you not to call me."

"I know what you said, but unfortunately, I don't always listen. Can I stop by your office tomorrow to see you? I have certain things on my mind, and I want to ask you some questions about investing the all-mighty dollar."

There was a long pause before he finally responded. "Your time will be limited." After that, he ended the call.

For now, I intended to take whatever time I could get.

The next day, I left the financial adviser's office around two o'clock and then headed to Charles's office. Like always, I made sure I looked good, smelled like a bed of roses, and was at my best. I strutted into his office, looking like a movie star. Heads turned as I asked the receptionist to buzz him, and when he came to the lobby, we immediately stepped into a nearby boardroom that had a round mahogany table with eight chairs surrounding it. Charles sat down in one of the chairs, while I closed the door and stood by it.

"My first question to you is, why are you playing games with me?" I said. "You know I've wanted to see you again."

"I'm too old to play games. And a whole lot of people want to see me. I don't make myself available to everyone. You shouldn't, either."

"Trust me when I say I don't. But I do make exceptions for special people. Don't you?"

He looked at his watched, then shifted his attention back to me. "Don't I what? What did you say?"

Unfortunately, he wasn't paying me much attention, so I spoke louder. "I said, 'I do you make exceptions for special people. Don't you?'"

"I don't know of many special people, so no, I don't." He looked at his watch again.

"I guess with you constantly looking at your watch, that means you have somewhere to be and I need to hurry this up. Right?"

"Exactly. We've been in here for almost five minutes, and you still haven't told me the purpose of your ongoing calls."

"You know the purpose of my calls, so stop trying to pretend that you don't. I want to play with your sock again. I really and truly do miss it."

"My sock doesn't have time to play. And what would make you think that you can just snap your fingers and have it available to you?"

"Because I have it like that, that's why."

His brows rose, and he stood up. "There is only one person in this room who has that much power. Breaking news, baby. It's not you. It's me, and I say my sock is busy."

"What makes you think that you're the one with all the power? I'd like to know, and if you can spare five more minutes of your time, please tell me."

"I'll tell you in less than a minute. You're here because you want me. You want to feel me again, and if you do, the only way you're going to get what you want from me is if you get on your knees, crawl over here, and come get it. There's still no guarantee that I will switch the power to you, but you have to start somewhere."

I wasn't sure if he was joking or not, but he was out of his damn mind if he thought I was going to get on my knees and crawl to him for some dick. I hadn't met a man yet who made me want to do that, and even though he was top-notch, that was a no-no.

"You can't be serious, and if you are, I may have a few words for you that you may not like."

He walked toward the door, then opened it. "Words are just words. When you're ready to do as I asked, call me. If not, don't bother."

He left the room and was gone in a flash. It looked as if I wasn't going to be getting any more of the good stuff anytime soon. If I had to crawl for it, I definitely didn't need it.

I stopped at the mall to pick up a customized purse I had ordered, and then I stopped to get some groceries. I thought about Trina not calling me back, and it made me kind of mad that she had cut me off earlier and hadn't even called back to apologize. That was just how things were in my world. I felt as if it was time to start removing more people from my circle. Cedric and Kayla were already gone, and Trina was the next one on my list. Instead of moving to a new town house, what I should've done was moved out of town. I needed to get away from everyone, and not even a seven-day trip would do me much good.

When I got home, I threw a TV dinner in the oven, popped some popcorn, and then prepared to watch a movie on Netflix. I was thirty minutes in when someone knocked on the door. There were only two people who knew where I lived. Either it was Trina or Kayla, obviously here to cause more trouble. I guessed Evelyn hadn't gotten the message from yesterday, when I had told her what I'd do if she didn't cut the crap. I meant every word.

I went to my bedroom to get my gun before going to the door. When I asked who was there, there was no answer. I looked through the peephole, and that was when I saw a big white man standing outside my door.

"Yes?" I said. "I think you're at the wrong door."

The man didn't budge. He knocked again, and when I pulled the door open, he looked me up and down.

"Mr. Washington wants to see you. You have to leave now."

A frown covered my face. I didn't have to do anything, and if Mr. Washington wanted to see me, then he'd better come here. I didn't mean to display an attitude, but what in the hell was going on here?

"Please let Mr. Washington know that I'm in the middle of watching a movie. If he wants to make arrangements to see me, then he needs to call me in advance."

The strong man lifted me and threw me over his shoulder. He reached for my door to shut it, and as I kicked, screamed, and hollered out in my pajamas, he put his hand over my mouth. He tossed me in the back of a black Escalade and then closed the door. He sped off, and when I kept asking him where he was taking me, he ignored me. I tried to unlock the doors, but to no avail. I screamed, "Help!" and banged on the windows, but it did me no good. I finally calmed down a little when I realized that the Escalade was on the way to Charles's office, or to his bunker, I should say.

Several minutes later, the man parked in the garage. When he opened the car door, I slowly got out. Taking the same route as I had with Charles, I found myself deep in the bunker and waiting for the man to get access by entering a code. When the doors opened, I followed him inside. He pointed toward a room.

"In there," he said, then walked away.

I made my way toward the room, and when I opened the door, Charles was there all by his lonesome self. He was sitting on a long sofa, with no clothes on. The room was rather dim, but I could see a bottle of champagne to his left and an array of stronger alcohol to his right.

"You know," he said, "I've been kind of thinking that that one little, measly time we spent together just wasn't enough. And since you keep calling and showing up at my job, I thought that maybe if I give you another chance to show me what you can really do with this, you'll decide to step up to the plate. The thing is, though, my comment from earlier still stands. If you want it, there is only one way to get it."

The whole time Charles spoke, my eyes were focused on his muscle, which rested on his leg. I had dreamed about being with him again, and all kind of thoughts had swum in my head about what I would do if or when I was given another opportunity.

"I have a problem with getting on my knees and crawling to you, and I also have a problem with you sending someone to my home to get me. How do you know where I live, if I haven't told you?"

"I always know where those special people are in my life, and even though I wasn't willing to admit it earlier, you are, indeed, special, Evelyn. Real special."

I didn't want to waste much more time on this, simply because I was so ready to tear into this man. And since he'd met me halfway by sending someone to my home to get me, I figured I could meet him halfway too. I dropped to my knees, and then I slowly crawled over to him. He watched, leaning slightly to his left, with his index finger against his temple. His eyes were narrowed, and his dick grew longer with every inch forward that I took. When I reached him, I maneuvered my body in between his legs. He sat up straight and then lifted my pajama top over my head. I was naked underneath. He cupped my exposed ass with his hands and squeezed it.

"This is it, Evelyn. Make it count for something."

I tried my best to do just that, but once again, I found myself being beaten down and defeated by Charles's dick. He tore me up on that sofa, and as he bent me over the back of it, I was punished for not abiding by his rules.

"No more, baby. You hear me?" he said, spewing his words while grinding way deep in the jungle. "This is it, and the next time I give you some of this, I'm going to make you pay for it."

"Whatever you want," I couldn't help saying, as I was on the verge of an orgasm. "You . . . you keep fucking me this good, and you can have whatever you want."

"I know. That's because I have the power, don't I?"

"Hell, yes, you do. All of it and then some."

He slapped my ass hard and then turned up the heat when he squatted behind me to catch my fluids in his mouth. I damn near jumped over the sofa, but he held my legs to stop me.

"Don't fly away until tomorrow," he said. "For the next few hours, you're mine."

Yes, I was his, and after he was done with me, he called his driver and had him take me home. I was in a daze as I walked through the door and bumped into a wall. My hair was a mess, my whole body was sweating, yet my pussy was so pleased. I lay on the sofa, cuddling my pillow. The only thought that was embedded in my brain was, *Charles*.

14

Trina

My heart started to beat faster, and I was totally speechless, after Keith asked how my trip to New York was. Did he make a mistake, or did he really know I had gone to New York to see Sasha? I had to pretend that I didn't know what he was talking about, because I simply wasn't prepared for this.

"New York? You mean Vegas."

"I didn't stutter. I said New York. You went to New York, not Vegas."

My face fell, cracked, and shattered into a thousand pieces. I opened my mouth, but nothing came out.

"I'ma give you time to think about how to approach this," he said. "Meet me at home."

He walked away and got into his car. After he drove off, I put my things in the trunk, then got inside my car. On the drive home, I was a nervous wreck. I had to tell him the truth about everything, and that included my feelings for Sasha, which had been all washed away. I felt like a complete fool. Keith didn't deserve this. If I lost him over this, I didn't know what I would do.

I parked my car in front of the house, and as soon as I entered, I saw numerous trash bags at the door. I could also tell that many of my belongings were inside the bags, and that made me ill. My stomach hurt so badly. I wanted to throw up, because I couldn't believe that while

I was in New York, he was here packing my shit. I turned to address him as he sat, with a twisted face, in the living room.

"What is this?" I said, pointing at the bags. "Are you putting me out of here? Is that what you're doing?"

"You're damn right I am. You don't belong here, Trina, and shame on me for thinking that you did."

Now, that hurt. I swallowed the lump in my throat and did my best to clean this up quickly.

"Okay, look. I'm sorry for not telling you about my trip to New York, but I was sure that you wouldn't understand. Every time I brought it up, it seemed as if you weren't interested in hearing about it. It's like you don't think my work is worthy of being on display, and Sasha was telling me all the things I needed to hear."

"That's bullshit, Trina, and you know it. Don't you stand there and blame me for your lies, especially when you know damn well that I wouldn't have had any problem with you going to New York if it were strictly about business."

"It was about business. That's why I went."

He looked at me as if he wanted to get up from that chair and choke the life out of me. I was holding back on saying much more. I didn't want this situation to turn ugly, and I damn sure didn't want him to put me out of here. I had no money, nor did I have anyplace to go.

"You know what gets me?" he said.

Right then, my phone rang, and it was Kayla. I hurried to answer, just in case I had to go to her for a place to stay. Sounding very unstable, she asked if I had Evelyn's address. I told her I would text it to her, since Keith was starting to get louder in the background. I ended the call and quickly texted the address to her.

"You thought I was that damn stupid," he went on to say. "Do you really believe that? You paraded around here like everything was all good, made your secretive phone calls, thinking that I was asleep. Then you told me every lie that you could possibly tell me to make me think you were going on a trip with Evelyn and Kayla. If that wasn't enough, and through all your deception, you had the audacity to tell me you loved me. What in the hell kind of love is that?"

It was apparent that he knew more than I had thought he knew. I walked into the living room and tried to explain what I'd done.

"I do love you. I have always loved you, but sometimes, it feels as if it's not enough. I'm still a little confused about certain things, and there are times when I do feel attracted to women. I didn't intend to act on those feelings, until Sasha called me out of the blue and started talking about helping me. Our conversations took a turn in another direction, and when she asked me to come see her, I felt as if I should go and work through these feelings inside of me, and also see what I could do to enhance my career."

Keith chuckled, then shook his head. "You sound like a damn fool. And you've been confused since I met you. I asked you to marry me, but you can't, because you're confused. I asked you to have my children, but you can't, because you're confused. I asked you to move in with me, and even though you evidently did, your initial reaction was that you couldn't, because you were confused. You're damn right you are confused. And a confused woman should not be living here with me. So, I have taken it upon myself to pack your bags and allow you to go find yourself. Take some time to figure out who or what you really want. Right now it's apparent that it's not me."

Tears started to well up in my eyes. This shit hurt, especially since I had to admit that it was all on me. I couldn't blame him for anything, not one single thing, and he had every right to be angry with me. I moved closer to him and knelt down in front of him as I attempted to make my case.

"I know what I want. I don't need to go figure out anything else, and I'm staying right here with you. We're going to work through this, Keith. I'm not letting you walk away from me, and that is something I am sure of."

"You weren't so sure when you happily walked your ass out of here and went to New York. I watched you these past few weeks with so much pain and hurt in my heart. Even while we were in New York, I saw the way you and Sasha looked at each other. I noticed how there was something sparking between the two of you, and I get tired of going places with you, and you are looking at women harder than me. From day one, I knew what you were plotting to do. I didn't say one word, because I wanted to know how far you would go. The last thing I want is a sneaky-ass woman. I'm not doing this with you, Trina. I can't ignore how much this is affecting me, and as far as I can see, we have no future."

His words stung. I dropped my head on his lap and started to cry. He knew that it took a lot for me to express my emotions, but I couldn't hold back. I needed Keith more than he ever knew. And while he was so right about my attraction to women, it didn't mean that I didn't want to be with him. It didn't mean that I wasn't in love with him. I loved him with all my heart. It was just that I had needed a little more time to explore what was inside me. Only a little. And after going to see Sasha, I knew that being with another woman was not where I wanted to be.

"Don't say that to me," I sobbed. "We do have a future, and I can't lose you, Keith. I can't, and you've got to understand why I did what I did."

"Thanks for letting me know that you fucked her."

He shoved me away from him and stood up. As he tried to walk away from me, I tugged at his arm. I begged and pleaded for him to give us another chance.

"Please, Keith. I did not have sex with her. I promise you I didn't. You have to believe me."

"Believe you? After you've been doing all of this lying to me? Woman, please. I don't believe shit you say, and you'll say anything just to stay in this house, living confused."

He snatched his arm away from me and started walking. I called after him, but he ignored me and jogged up the stairs. I followed behind him, with so much hurt in my eyes. I was disappointed that I couldn't get through to him. He walked into the bedroom.

"Will you please listen to me?" I said, entering the bedroom. "What do I need to say for you to listen to me?"

"You don't have to say anything. Now, I've been nice and very calm about this. In a minute, I'm going to lose it. I want you out of here, Trina. Nothing else needs to be said."

I stood and looked at him without saying a word. He turned his head to look in another direction. I knew I could get through to him, but he was so stubborn at times.

"Keith, I'm begging you not to end this with me. I will marry you. I will have your children, I will do whatever it is that you need me to do. But what I need is for you to forgive me. Please forgive me, and don't do this to us."

He shook his head in disgust, plopped on the bed, and kept massaging his hands. "Now you want to marry me. Now you want to have my baby. This is some funny shit, Trina, and you must really think I'm a damn fool. Go marry your girlfriend in New York. Go fuck her some more, and just maybe, maybe she can help you with your career."

"I did not fuck her!" I screamed. "All we did was kiss, and that was it! I didn't want to go any further with her, because I wasn't feeling her like that! It was a big mistake, and I'm so, so sorry!"

"Don't raise your goddamned voice at me, especially after you're the one out there, fucking cheating on me! And you didn't make no mistake. What you did was fuck up." His voice went up a notch.

I could tell my time was running out.

"You fucked up, Trina, and you won't get another chance!" He got off the bed and stood directly in front of me. My head was lowered, but he lifted my chin so I could look at him. "You know why you don't get another chance? Because your lies already caused one of your bitches to put a knife in me. Your lies almost killed me before, and your lies had me lying up in a hospital bed for three weeks, not knowing if I would ever be right again. I'm not going to sit here and wait for another one of your bitches to come and attack me. There was something in Sasha's eyes that told me she didn't have all her marbles. You didn't notice that, because you were too busy trying to figure out when and where you wanted to fuck her. But you know what? My thanks go to ole dad once again for confirming everything that I needed to know."

Keith had it all figured out. With Mr. Washington working for the government and somehow or someway being affiliated with the CIA, it wasn't hard for Keith to get ahold of my phone records, bank records, flight information, whatever he needed. I felt horrible, and at this point, there was nothing else I could say.

"Now, Trina," he said, "it's time for you to go."

I tried to swallow the oversize lump in my throat, which felt stuck. It wouldn't go away, so I wiped my tears and then pivoted away from him. My legs were so weak that I could barely walk down the stairs. And when he slammed the bedroom door behind me, my whole body shook. One by one, I carried the trash bags containing my possessions to my car. And just as I grabbed the last bag, my phone rang again. This time, it was Evelyn. I was so frustrated that I put down the bag, answered the call, and yelled at her.

"What is it? I'm busy right now. I'll have to call you back!"

I threw my phone down, almost breaking it. This was not good for me, and I knew it. I looked up the stairs and softly called Keith's name.

"Are you listening to me?" I said. "I hope you are, because all I can say to you right now is that I love you. With all my heart, I truly do."

Unfortunately, there was no response, so I left, taking the last bag out of Keith's house.

I drove around in my car for what seemed like hours, thinking about what had just happened and trying to figure out where I should go. I could probably go stay with either one of my BFF's, but I didn't feel like discussing all that had happened today. Instead, I pulled my car over to the curb and cried my ass off. I wound up falling asleep, and when I woke up, it was morning. I wiped my mouth and then decided to go to Evelyn's place, instead of Kayla's. Jacoby was still living there, and I didn't want to inconvenience two people. I was sure that Evelyn would have her gripes too, but when she opened the door at her place, she had a smile on her face.

"Come in and tell me what happened," she said. "Did Kayla tell you about our fight? I hope you're not mad at me, because that was her fault, not mine."

"I—I don't know what you're talking about. I haven't spoken to Kayla. I'm here because when I got back from New York yesterday, Keith put me out."

"What?" she shouted as I walked inside and plopped down on the sofa. "Why did he put you out? Then again, never mind. I warned you, Trina. I warned you about this, and I told you that going to New York wasn't a good idea."

"I know, and I made one big fool of myself. All Sasha wanted to do was have sex. She lied about people wanting to help me. Nobody wanted to help me. All she wanted to do was help herself."

"Duuuh! You didn't know that? Some women are just as bad as men. You have to be careful out there. You're lucky that she didn't cut yo' ass up and leave you in a trash can somewhere, stinking. I'm surprised that you fell for her games, Trina. This is not like you. What exactly were you thinking?"

"I know. Crazy, right? That's why I'm so mad at myself. Keith is never going to forgive me, and he made that perfectly clear."

"It is a hard pill to swallow, but how did he know you went to New York? And whatever you do, don't go pointing the finger at me. Everybody wants to blame me, and I assure you that I have not spoken to Keith."

"I'm not accusing you of anything. I'm sure he did some little investigations on his own, but I'm also sure that his dad gave him some information too."

"How could his dad give him information about you? He doesn't know you like that, does he?"

I sat silent for a few seconds; then I spoke up. "He knows everything about everything, in case you didn't know that. The man works for the government, and without going into details, he is privy to a lot of information."

Evelyn's eyes bugged out. "Is he really CIA? I knew there was something about him, because don't no regular person have access to underground bunkers."

"Bunkers? What are you talking about?"

"I'm talking about going underground to work and do other great things. It's where he takes me to screw my brains out, and I must say that last night was spectacular."

I shook my head, then massaged it, because it hurt. "Evelyn, you need to stop. I don't think you should make a move in that direction, and I'm just telling you that for your own good."

"Yeah, like I tried to tell you about going to New York. You didn't listen to me, so please don't sit there and tell me what I should or shouldn't do. With that being said, I guess you came here because you need a place to stay. I don't mind you staying here, but even though this place is paid for, I still want you to contribute something. It's out of respect, if you know what I mean."

"That's nice of you, and thanks for letting me stay here. I can honestly say that this is a side of you that I could get used to."

"I'm not all that bad, trust me. Besides, I do get lonely over here sometimes. It'll be good to have you around. But please don't overstay your welcome."

"I won't. As soon as I can figure out a way to get back on my feet, or get back into Keith's house, I'm out."

"I don't know how long that will be, and if he's stubborn like his father is, you could be in for a long wait."

Evelyn and I started to talk about how she had got hooked up with Charles. We also talked about the fight between her and Kayla. I was stunned. I wanted to believe that she was telling the truth, and if I had to put my money on her instead of Cedric, I would. His dirty ass was out to destroy our friendship and everything about us. I wasn't sure if Kayla was aware of that or not, but since Evelyn said she thought Cedric had jumped on Kayla, maybe she was starting to open her eyes.

"I still haven't spoken to her," I said. "I've had a lot going on myself, but I was going to call her. I don't want to suggest that we all get together and talk, but sooner or later, we're going to have to get together and do something about Cedric. He is out of control, and he should be arrested."

"I agree one hundred percent. But Kayla is the one who holds the key. She needs to deal with him fast."

Maybe she would, and if it was true about him putting his hands on her, I was sure that Kayla had something in store for him.

15

Kayla

I had been so drunk that I could barely see straight. All I remembered was stumbling and then falling on the floor and almost hitting my head. Jacoby had said something to me, but I hadn't been able to make out what it was. I hadn't cared. At this point, I didn't care about anything. I hated my life, and I had to figure out a way to escape from it.

What Cedric did to me had left me bitter and angry. It had got me to a point where I wanted to remove him from this earth and this time get it right. With him being gone, Jacoby wouldn't have to worry anymore about going to jail. I wouldn't have to worry anymore, and he would be out of our lives for good. The more I looked at my face in the mirror, the angrier I got. I had to do this, and if it meant jail time for me, so be it. I already felt as if I was living in hell. All the money in the world wasn't enough to take away this pain, and it sure the hell didn't make me happy.

Now, hours later, I crawled on the floor, removing myself from the vomit I lay in. It felt like someone was beating a hammer against my head, so I sluggishly walked toward the bathroom to take some aspirin. Afterward, I removed my soiled clothes, then took a hot shower. Once I was done, I changed into some clean clothes and made my way back into the living room area to clean up my mess. As I was on my knees, scrubbing the carpet with a towel, Jacoby walked up to me.

"What happened to your face?" he said. "How did it get like that?"

"Do you have to ask? I was so drunk that I can't remember. All I know is I had a hard fall last night and I hurt myself."

"Did you go see Cedric?"

Yet again, I found myself lying, because I didn't want Jacoby to know that Cedric had done this to me. The last thing I needed was for him to go over to Cedric's place. I was sure—no, positive—that Cedric would do the same thing to Jacoby as he had done to me and Justin.

"No. I called him, but he refused to talk to me. I guess when things settle down, we'll talk."

"Or I'll go talk to him myself."

"No!" I shouted, then calmed my voice. "I don't want you to do that now. You saw how Cedric acted the other day. He knows something, and I fear that he may hurt you."

"Yeah, well, I'm not afraid of him anymore. He and I need to have a talk, and it's time that you moved out of the way and let that happen."

I was getting frustrated with Jacoby. He just didn't know when to listen. If he thought for one minute that Cedric was going to embrace him with open arms, he was sadly mistaken. That simply wasn't going to happen.

I threw the dirty towel on the carpet, then looked at him. "I've been in the way because I'm your mother, and you're all that I have. I can't just sit back and do nothing, Jacoby. I do hope that you understand that, and if you do, please listen to me and forget about going to see Cedric."

"I do understand, but you're losing yourself. Look at you, Mama. You're a mess. I get tired of coming in here almost every night and seeing you passed out on the floor and laying in your vomit. When are you going to stop this?"

I stood up and put my hands on my hips. "If you get tired of coming in here and seeing me like this every night, then your solution is simple. Don't come home. If it's that bad, Jacoby, you really don't have to be here."

"I agree. That's why I'm moving in with Adrianne and her mother for a while. I get way more peace there than I do here."

He had just pissed me off without even knowing it. Sometimes kids said the wrong things when they should have just kept their mouths shut.

"Fine, Jacoby. Go ahead and run your tail to your girlfriend's house. They have the perfect life over there, and you'll fit right in."

He shrugged his shoulders, then walked away from me. Minutes later, he came back downstairs. I was in the kitchen, drinking water. A heavy duffel bag was on his shoulder, and a pair of his tennis shoes was in his hands.

"I'll check in with you later," he said.

I rolled my eyes and tried my best not to show how hurt I was. Funny how when he needed me, I was there for him. But when I needed him, he walked.

"Don't bother, Jacoby. No need to bother."

He walked away, and when the door slammed, I was crushed. I went right over to the liquor cabinet and snatched a whole bottle of whiskey from the shelf. I opened it, and as I started to guzzle it down, the liquid ran down my chin and spilled all over my clothes. I gagged and then threw the bottle so hard that it cracked on my kitchen floor. Shards of glass were everywhere.

I went into the living room and fell back on the sofa, wondering how in the hell a woman like me had got here. The first thing that came into my head was, *Lies*. Maybe, just maybe, if I had told Cedric the truth about Jacoby not being his son, we wouldn't even be here. Maybe if I had told him about Jacoby trying to kill him, we wouldn't even be here. While I didn't take responsibility for him cheating on me, I had to know that some of this was on me too. Still, it was too late to fix it. I had helped to create that monster. I sat for a while, thinking about how to disable it. I got a little help when Cedric called with some more of what he called "breaking news."

"I slept on what happened over here, and I called to say I'm sorry. Sorry for not taking action sooner. Before the end of the week, *your* son will be arrested. I'm gathering all the information Evelyn and Paula have provided me with. Once I have my ducks in a row, lives will change."

He hung up, leaving it right there. That was the last straw. I stumbled into my bedroom, changed my wet shirt, which reeked of alcohol, and then reached for the gun underneath my bed. In that moment, I was so mad at Paula for not doing away with Cedric when she had the chance to. *Damn her*. Why did she leave it up to me to finish the job? I had to be the one to finish this, and no matter what, I would get it right.

I stood up straight, with no fear in me whatsoever. I tucked the gun in my purse, then took one last swig of alcohol from a bottle in the liquor cabinet before heading out the door. I rushed to get into my car and headed to Cedric's place, which was only several minutes away. I was speeding so fast through my neighborhood that I could hear my tires making a whooshing sound. And just as I was about to make a right onto the main street, I saw a little girl run into the street to go after her ball.

I gasped, then slammed on the brakes. My tires screeched loudly, and my whole body jerked forward. I looked up and saw that the front of my car was within inches—only inches—of the little girl's body. She cried loudly as her mother charged out into the street and let me have it. With her daughter clinging to her, she pounded the hood of my car with her fists, overcome by much rage and anger.

"You stupid bitch!" she yelled. "Didn't you see her? Why in the hell were you driving so fast! Slow the hell down! Nothing is that damn important where you have to almost kill my freaking child!"

She was so right. I dropped my head on the steering wheel and broke down. This was definitely God's way of trying to save me. He had put a little girl in my way to stop me. I needed help, and I needed it now.

16

Evelyn

In my world, everything seemed to be going well. My financial adviser had shared some good ideas with me about increasing my wealth, and I had taken heed of everything he said. I had left an enormous amount of money in the bank, and I had also given Trina a few thousand dollars to help get her back on her feet. She was a total mess. I had never seen her this emotional, and it was kind of strange to see her crying all the time. I wanted her and Keith to work things out, and even though he would never, ever listen to me, I decided to stop by his house and tell him exactly what Trina had been going through. Maybe he would understand and decide to give her another chance.

I arrived at Keith's house at a little after four that afternoon. Lord knows, I hated the cold weather, and it was starting to turn cold. A gusty wind blew my hair all over my head as I headed up the sidewalk to his front door, and I could see just a little snow starting to fall. This was crazy because it was only early October. Winter hadn't officially arrived yet, but St. Louis weather was always tricky like that.

I rang the doorbell, and minutes later, through the window I could see Keith coming down the stairs in jeans and a T-shirt. Unfortunately for Trina, a female trailed right behind him. She looked okay, but quite frankly, she didn't have anything on Trina. I wasn't sure who she was, but when he opened the door, she made an exit.

"Thanks, Keith," she said. "You are totally the bomb. I'll keep in mind what you said."

"You do that, and I'll see you again tomorrow."

The nappy-headed bitch didn't even speak to me. Just walked right past me as if I wasn't even standing there. I swore that some people were just so rude. Either way, I flashed a smile at Keith, but his expression was flat.

"Why are you here, Evelyn?"

"Trina is at my place, and I need to talk to you about her. May I come in?"

"Talking to me about Trina will do you no good. I don't want you to waste your time."

"Aw, come on, Keith. People get cheated on all the time, and they learn to forgive. You know Trina loves you. She just made a mistake, and the last time I checked, we all make them."

"Yeah, we do. And you should know all about those mistakes, Evelyn. Especially since you keep on making them. I honestly can't wait until you get yours. You are so deserving of all that you have coming, and you're too blind to see that an earthquake is coming your way. The last thing you need to concern yourself with is my relationship with Trina. What you need to concern yourself with is your relationship with my father. I hear it's been fun, but all good things do come to an end."

I guessed Trina must have told him about me seeing his father, even though she'd said she wouldn't. I suspected that it would just be a matter of time before I heard from his mother, or maybe he hadn't said anything to her yet. He was probably on Team Dad, and this was their little secret too.

"I am having a lot of fun with him, and during the process, I am still concerned about my friend. Don't let a good woman pass you by, Keith. All she did was kiss the darn girl and exchange a few feels with her. You act like she went all the way with her. And when it comes to lies, we have all had to fib a little. You're not perfect, and you shouldn't expect her to be perfect, either."

"Evelyn, talking to you is a waste of time. I have work to do, so good-bye."

"Yeah, whatever. But what am I supposed to tell Trina in the meantime? I at least want to give her some hope. Is there anything you would like for me to say to her?"

He stroked his chin, as if he was in thought, then snapped his fingers. "As a matter of fact, there is. I've been doing a lot of thinking over these past few days, thinking about what I would say to her if I saw her. That would be . . . to go to hell. You can go there too."

Well, damn, I thought when he slammed the door in my face. Through the window I saw him jog back up the stairs. *Vicious and nasty*. He was beyond mad at Trina. I hadn't known he was that serious. If Trina was ever going to call this place home again, she had her work cut out for her.

I returned home, only to find Trina weeping as she lay in the guest bedroom. I guessed when you realized how badly you had fucked up, it was a hard pill to swallow. I sat next to her on the bed, then pulled her to me.

"Stop this, okay?" I said. "I know it hurts, but you have to know that what is meant to be will be. Keith isn't the only good man out there, and you are not a bad person. Still a little confused, though." I laughed. "But certainly not a bad person. Stop beating yourself up about what you did."

Trina dabbed her eyes with a tissue and then sat up straight. "I miss him," she said. "I miss him so much, Evelyn. I don't know what I'm going to say or do to get him back."

I didn't want to go there, but I had to get Trina up and out of this bed and energized to get her man back.

"Well, you won't get him back by staying in bed all day, crying. If you don't get up, there are plenty of women out there, ready to make a move. I ran into one chick as I went by his house today to talk to him. I was only trying to help, but there was someone else there with him."

Trina cocked her head back. "Who?" she said. "What did she look like?"

"She was kind of tall, had short hair and some really wide hips. She mentioned something about him helping her, and he told her that he would see her again tomorrow."

"That must have been Latisha. She comes by sometimes so that he can help her with her paintings. I have never trusted that hoochie, though, and if she knows I'm out of the picture, she will definitely do whatever to slide right in."

"Hell, who wouldn't? On a scale from one to ten, it ain't like Keith a five. That man is ten all the way, and I'm not just talking about his looks."

"Ten and then some," Trina said softly. "It's funny how you see a clear picture when you've broken up with somebody. All I can think about is where I went wrong."

"Yes, wrong, wrong, wrong. And you were also wrong for telling Keith about me and his father. I wanted you to do so, but I didn't expect for Keith to mention it today."

Trina had a puzzled look on her face. "He knows? I didn't say one word to him about you messing with his father. I was going to, but I decided against it."

Now we both looked puzzled. "If he does know, who told him?" I said. "I just can't see his father telling him anything like that, especially since he made it clear that I'd better not open my mouth."

"I don't know. I can't see him telling Keith, either."

I got off the bed and headed to the door. "The only way to find out is for me to call Mr. Washington and see who's been talking."

I went into the kitchen to get my purse and cell phone. When I punched in his number, he answered on the third ring. I didn't even get a chance to say hello.

"Evelyn, this is the last call you will ever make to me. Good-bye."

"But wait!" I shouted. "Why did you tell Keith about us? You know he knows, don't you? I'm just trying to warn you."

The call ended. I called back but didn't get through, and after I tried several more times to reach him, with no success, I spoke with the operator, who said the phone number had been disconnected. I couldn't believe it had been disconnected that fast. I was so curious, and I needed some answers. He could stop me from calling him, but he couldn't stop me from being face-to-face with him. I rushed to the guest bedroom and told Trina I was leaving.

"Where are you going?" she said.

"I'll be right back. I need to go see someone."

"Who? Mr. Washington?"

"Yes."

"I want to go. I'll stay in the car or whatever, but I just need to get out of here."

I was hesitant. After all, I didn't want Trina around, just in case he wanted me to crawl for him again. But I also knew that Charles was a late-night lover. He liked to wait until business hours were over to do his dirt. Then again, so did I.

"Come on, Trina. Hurry up and put on some clothes. I'll wait for you in the car."

Trina got out of the bed, and I went to my car. I even called Charles's phone one more time, just to be sure that it was disconnected. It was.

Minutes later, Trina came outside, looking like a slouchy bum in an oversized shirt and pants. It was a good thing that we weren't going to see Keith, with her looking like that. And wherever we ultimately wound up going, I had to be sure that she stayed in the car.

I drove to Charles's office, and after I parked, I told Trina that I would be right back. She yawned, then laid her head back on the headrest.

"Don't be too long. And after we leave here, can we please go get something to eat? I'm hungry."

"Me too, but be patient. I'll be back as soon as I can."

I closed the car door and then went inside the building. Something about this day felt really strange to me, and when I got off the elevator, went up to the receptionist, and asked to speak with Charles, she told me he didn't work there.

"Excuse me," I said to the receptionist, whom I had never seen before today. "I know he works here. I've come here to see him many times before."

"I'm sorry, ma'am. You must have the wrong floor. There is no Charles Washington in this office."

"Do you mind if I go back to the office where I normally meet him at? I can go get him for you. I think that since you're new, you don't know who he is."

"No, I've been working here for almost four years. I was on vacation for a few weeks, but I can assure you that no Mr. Charles Washington has ever worked here."

I scratched my head, and a look of anger washed over my face. I wasn't sure if I would get myself in trouble or not, but I rushed away from the desk and stormed down the hallway. I could see Charles's office from a distance, and as the receptionist called after me, I kept going. I quickly opened the door and stepped inside the room. There were four white men in suits standing in the office, talking business. Three were sitting in chairs, while the other one was standing and pointing to a diagram on the wall.

"May I help you?" said the one who was standing.

"I—I'm looking for Mr. Charles Washington. This is his office, isn't it? Is he here?"

"Charles who?" the man asked, with a disturbing look on his face. "No, this is my office, and I don't know him."

I thought I was going crazy. I walked out the door, and when I slowly walked past the receptionist, with a bewildered look on my face, I barely heard what she said.

"Leave now, or I'll call security."

I walked to the elevator, feeling numb. What in the hell was going on? Surely, I was at the right building and on the right floor. There was no way that they didn't know Charles. Instead of going back to the car, I got on the elevator and hit the button for the lower level, where the bunker was located. But as I made my exit, I discovered that there was a wall to my left and a wall to my right. Short hallways were on both sides, but that was it. I could go no farther, and in that moment, I truly felt as if I had lost my mind. Just to confirm that I hadn't, I went back to the car to question Trina.

"Something really strange just happened in there," I told her after I climbed in the front seat. I was still in awe. "They told me Charles doesn't work here. I went to his office, and he wasn't there."

"Did he quit or something? Maybe he quit."

"No. The receptionist told me he has never worked there. That was a total lie, and you know it. You yourself said that you and Keith brought him something here before, didn't you?"

"Yes, we did. He used to work here, and whoever told you he didn't was lying."

"Yeah, there seems to be a lot of that going on lately. And all I can say is, something doesn't feel right, Trina. All of a sudden Keith knows about me and his father, but you didn't tell him. Not to mention that he didn't tell you he knew. I don't like the feeling of this, and I'm starting to feel real weird."

"I agree that something isn't adding up, but it could be that Charles just doesn't want to have anything else to do with you. Men get like that, and it may be to the point where he's trying to protect his marriage. I'm sure you call and bug him a lot, Evelyn. I know how you are, and you can be quite demanding."

"Yeah, whatever, but it still doesn't explain the whole bunker thing. That bunker in the basement is gone. It has a whole new look down there. You can go see for yourself."

"I've never seen this bunker you're talking about, but I do know that Mr. Washington has worked here before. I'll let you figure out what is going on, and I'm sure the two of you will be in touch soon."

I started the car, with a puzzled look locked on my face. I wasn't so sure that Trina believed everything I'd said, but I had to be clear that I wasn't crazy. "You don't think I'm crazy, do you, Trina?"

"I'm not saying that you are crazy, Evelyn. What I've said all along is that you shouldn't be messing with Mr. Washington. He's a real private man, and to be honest with you, whenever I've been around him, it has kind of scared me. He's too darn observant. Looks as if he's studying people all the time and taking notes in his head. He makes me nervous, even though he is a nice man. I honestly do not know if he's in some way connected with the CIA or not. Keith has never confirmed that either way. But I do know that he has a lot of power and influence in our city. That, I can confirm."

I thought back to when Charles got pulled over by the police. Shit was starting to make sense to me, and I couldn't help but wonder how this was going to unfold.

17

Trina

Evelyn and I ate dinner together at a restaurant, but the whole time she appeared to be in a daze. She picked at her salad and kept staring off into space. I waved my hand in front of her face, in hopes that she would snap out of it.

"Come back, come back from wherever you are," I said.

She shot back a fake smile. "I'm sorry. I can't help myself. My thoughts are all over the place right now."

"They should be. And I hope you're coming to the conclusion, like I have, that you shouldn't have gone there with Mr. Washington."

"I don't know how I feel about it right now. The outcome of this has yet to be seen. I'm sure I'll hear from him, and whenever I do, he's going to get an earful."

Evelyn told me about the white man coming to her door and whisking her away to the bunker. I myself was starting to feel not so good about this. Was there a chance that Evelyn was lying? Yes, Mr. Washington did work in the building we had gone to. But something wasn't adding up. All this talk about bunkers, limos, and overly big dicks wasn't quite clicking with me. Evelyn's mother had a history of mental illness. A tiny part of me was starting to think that it had rubbed off. I didn't dare say that to her.

By nine o'clock that night, we were done eating and on our way back home. When we got back to her place, Evelyn parked her car, and then she popped the trunk.

"I put a trash bag in my trunk earlier," she said, in a somber mood. "I forgot to take it to the Dumpster, so I'm taking it now. Here are my keys to let yourself in."

"I'll take the trash to the Dumpster. Go inside and lie down. You look like you could use some rest."

She released a deep sigh. "Yes, I could. Thanks, Trina. I really appreciate it."

She walked toward her town house, and with the trash bag in hand, I made my way to the Dumpster, thinking about my BFF's. We were seriously going through some things. But we always had a problem rallying around each other for support. Either Kayla was mad at me or at Evelyn. Or she was mad at both of us, or I was in no mood to be around them. We had to do better than this, and even though I didn't want to force anything on either of them, we had to try again to work things out. I wasn't giving up on my friends, and the truth of the matter was this: we were all we had.

I dumped the trash and then made my way back to Evelyn's town house. From a short distance away, I heard something like moaning going on. I thought someone was having sex in a car, until I approached Evelyn's door. When I opened it, there she was on the hallway floor, with her skirt flipped up and Cedric on top of her. His hand was clamped over her mouth, and she was squirming around on the floor, moaning something and trying to get away from him. He punched her in the stomach to try to get her to be still.

"You can't run from me, bitch! I know your every move, and I told you there would be consequences if you didn't do what I told you to do!" Cedric yelled.

I was shocked by what I saw. I had never witnessed Cedric in action like this, and I moved a little closer to make sure it was him. He didn't see me, but I was positive that Evelyn did. Her watery eyes, with mascara running from them, shifted to me. That was what made him turn around. Without saying one word, I picked up one of Evelyn's statues on a shelf in the hallway and slammed it against his head. The hard blow was enough to knock him out cold, and it damn sure caused him to get off of her. She crawled backward and then got up off the floor and rushed to her bedroom.

Cedric got up slowly, holding his head. His eyes fluttered a few times, and he peered at me with a devilish look in his eyes. "I . . . I've been waiting on a piece of you for a long time too," he said softly, then looked at the blood on his trembling fingers. Thick blood started to run slowly down the side of his face, and his eyes fluttered again. He looked dizzy, as if he was seconds away from collapsing and dying right in front of me.

Did I hit him that hard? I wondered. I started to get real, real nervous, and even more so when Evelyn appeared in the hallway with a gun in her hand.

"Get out, Cedric! And don't you ever bring your ass back here again!" she shouted.

He stumbled as he turned around and looked at her, and when they made eye contact, she moved closer and fired one bullet into his chest. His blood splattered all over her clothes. He fell forward, and as he leaned on her, she pumped two more bullets into his stomach. She growled, as if doing this hurt her more than the bullets hurt him.

"Die, bastard! Die!" she said through gritted teeth.

I was numb all over. Couldn't move, didn't breathe. Didn't take one step. Just stood there and watched Cedric's body hit the floor like a bloody piece of meat. My body trembled as I watched Evelyn. It was as if she were another person when that gun was in her hand. After she snapped out of it and began to fall apart, she dropped the gun and fell beside Cedric.

"OMG, Trina! What did I just do? Come help me with him. We've got to save him!" She spoke in a panic. As she struggled to turn Cedric's body over, it was obvious that he was, indeed, dead. "Help me!" Evelyn cried out. "What did I *do*?"

I stared at the huge gash on his head, knowing that my blow had probably mortally wounded him and that he would have died even if Evelyn hadn't shot him. I wasn't sure if Evelyn knew it too, until she looked at the gash and covered her mouth. She looked at me with wide eyes.

"Did this gash . . . how . . . what?" She was crying so hard, she could barely get out the words.

I finally snapped out of my trance and rushed over to them. "Should we call the police?" I blurted, all the while thinking about my situation and about going to jail. This was so fucked up. I couldn't believe how people's lives could change in an instant. I began to cry.

Evelyn ran her bloody fingers through her hair, pulling it back. "Uh, let me think. Let me think. Let me think about this." She looked at Cedric again, which caused her to cry harder. "Oh, my, God! What did we do to him, and what should we do?"

Both of us couldn't stop the tears. We were in a severe panic, and we definitely knew that someone had heard those gunshots.

"We have to get out of here," I said. "Let's get out of here and go . . . go somewhere and think. I can't stay in here with his body lying there like that." I slowly backed away from Cedric's body, and so did Evelyn.

"But we, we can't leave him here like this, can we?" she screamed. "Trina, damn it! We have to call the police!"

"Stop screaming, would you? We *will* call them, just not right now. Right now we need to think hard and come up with the best story that will help to clear us. This isn't good, Evelyn. Trust me when I say this isn't good."

She clawed at her chest and kept looking at Cedric's body. "I know this isn't good, but what if he's still alive? We need to call an ambulance and see if they can get here and save him."

I didn't know what Evelyn was thinking, but with his eyes opened wide like that, it was clear that Cedric was dead. He was gone, and there was no bringing him back this time.

"Calling an ambulance won't save him. And calling the police won't save us. We've got to lock up your place and go."

Finally, Evelyn agreed. She tiptoed over Cedric's body, washed her hands in the kitchen, and then snatched up a jacket to cover her bloody clothes. Hoping that no one saw us, after Evelyn locked the front door, we ran to my car.

"Where are we going?" she said.

"To Kayla's place. We've got to go there."

Evelyn seemed reluctant, and while we were in the car, she told me that she thought going to Kayla's was a bad idea. "Trina, Kayla would love to see me behind bars. I know she would, and I don't think we should go there."

"What makes you think that you'll be the one locked up? I think it was my blow that ultimately killed him. He was mortally wounded before you put those bullets into him."

She was quiet for a few minutes, as if she was pondering something. "You don't know that for sure. And even if you were the one who killed him, you can't go to jail. I won't let you do it. I won't let you take the blame."

I swallowed hard, thinking about my situation again. "I don't have a choice. What choice do I have?"

"We *do* have a choice, and the last thing you're going to do is have that baby in jail. He or she will need you, Trina. You can't be a mother to your child if you're in prison."

I didn't know how Evelyn knew I was pregnant, because I hadn't told anyone. She must have seen the pregnancy test in the trash bag.

"Yes, I know," she said. "I saw the pregnancy test. We have to figure out a way to spin this, and we have to do it real fast."

I couldn't even think straight. It was in our best interest to go somewhere and chill for a while. I couldn't think of a better place than Kayla's. I tried to convince Evelyn to go there with me.

"We have so much to explain to her. She doesn't know what you told me about Cedric, does she?" I said.

"I tried to tell her, but she didn't listen. If she didn't listen then, she won't listen now."

"Please, just follow my lead on this. Just this one time, Evelyn, do it."

Evelyn's legs kept shaking, and she didn't say another word. When we got to Kayla's place, she remained in the car.

"I'm not going in there, because all she'll want to do is fight me," she said. "I'm not in the mood for it, so I'm staying right here. You can go in there and talk to her."

"No, Evelyn, we both need to go inside. Please do this. I can't think of a better time for us to come together and figure out what to do."

Evelyn finally listened to me and went to Kayla's door with me. We knocked several times, and almost five minutes later, Kayla opened the door. She appeared calm, but there was no smile whatsoever on her face, especially as she looked at Evelyn.

"Trina, I told you not to do this," she said. "Don't bring her over here. All I want right now is peace."

"I do too, but . . . but something just happened that I think you need to know about. It's important, Kayla. I wouldn't be here like this if it wasn't."

Kayla let us inside, and when she turned on the light in the foyer, she finally saw some of the bloodstains on our clothes, especially on Evelyn's. Kayla covered her mouth, then stepped back.

"What happened?" she said in a high-pitched tone. "Where did all this blood come from?"

"Cedric," I didn't hesitate to say. "Cedric is dead."

Kayla's eyes bugged out. She took a few more steps back. "How . . . ? When? And who—"

"I'll tell you all about it, but I want you to come with us," I said. "Please come with us so that I can explain everything to you."

This time, it wasn't Evelyn who was hesitant. It was Kayla. "I'm not going anywhere. Tell me what is going on right now!"

Tears were on the brink of falling from her eyes. This was one gut-wrenching moment, but I needed Kayla, as well as Evelyn, to cooperate.

"Evelyn and I are going to be in big trouble," I said. "Cedric made us do this. He was like an out-of-control madman who couldn't be stopped. If you had seen him, you would know what I mean. We had to do something to stop him."

Something snapped Kayla out of her resistance mode. She opened the front door, then wiped away a tear that had fallen down her face. "I know what you mean, but take me to him," she said. "Tell me what happened in the car and take me to him."

I didn't want to go back there and stare at him again. But when I asked Kayla if we could just chill at her place for a few hours, she wasn't down with it.

"No, Trina. Let's go now. I want to see him. Staying here won't do us any good."

I didn't want to argue with Kayla, and neither did Evelyn. We all got in the car, and as I took a circuitous route back to Evelyn's place, just to waste more time, we gave Kayla more details about what had happened before and after this incident. I couldn't remember some of the missing pieces, so Evelyn spoke up and told Kayla everything. She spilled her guts about Cedric coming to the hospital, and about him forcing himself on her. She mentioned his threatening phone calls and her suspicions that he was trying to destroy our friendship. She also gave specific details about what had just happened at her town house. She made it seem as if her shooting him had killed him. I then told Kayla that I thought his death was due to what I'd done. Kayla was speechless the whole time we spoke.

There was a long silence before Kayla mentioned what Cedric had done to her. "I didn't know who he was," she said tearfully. "I never thought he would do me like that, and I'm still in shock about it."

Not only was she in shock then, but she was in complete and utter shock when she walked through the door of Evelyn's town house and saw Cedric's dead body lying there. At a slow pace, Kayla walked up to him and then fell to her knees.

"No, no, no!" she cried out. "How dare you do this! How dare you cause me so much pain and suffering and then lay your ass there and die!" She pounded his chest with her fists, causing it to rise a little.

I had no idea what was going through her head right now. She and Cedric had a long history together, and they had been together since college. As much as Kayla might have despised him, I was sure that it was hard on her to see him lying there like this. It was hard on all of us, and when Evelyn walked up to Kayla, she lost it.

"I am so sorry, my dear friend," Evelyn said softly. "I didn't want to kill him, but I had to. I had to do it, Kayla, and you just don't understand what kind of man Cedric was. Maybe with you he was different. With me, he wasn't. He treated me like shit, and I had my own reasons for accepting it. I wish I could bring him back. Lord knows, I wish I could, but I . . . I'm sorry."

Kayla didn't respond to Evelyn. She laid her head on Cedric's bloody chest, sobbing uncontrollably. All we could hear was her cries. Other than that, the room was silent. There was something in the air that sent chills all over my body. I wasn't sure if Evelyn or Kayla felt it, but I surely did. I stood there without moving, looked at my BFF's, who were torn beyond repair, and couldn't find the right words to say to either one of them. I just allowed them all the time and space they needed to get through this very frightening moment.

"What are we going to do?" Kayla finally said, with tears streaming down her face, as she looked from Evelyn to me. "We can't leave him lying here like this."

I stepped closer, but my legs were so weak that I could barely stand. "I guess we need to call the police. But what are we going to say?"

Evelyn sucked in a deep breath, then released it. "We're going to tell them that it was self-defense and that I shot him."

"But what about the gash on his head?" I questioned. "This doesn't look good, and I doubt that the police will believe it was self-defense."

Kayla slowly stood and started to wipe the tears from her face. "Trina is right. They're not going to buy that. I hate to say this, but I think we may need to take his body somewhere and dump it."

Evelyn's eyes bugged out. "Are you out of your mind!" she shouted. "We can't do that. Someone may see us, and if his body is ever found, we could all be facing jail time."

I agreed with Evelyn. "I don't like the idea of removing his body from here and dumping it somewhere. I do think we need to call the police, and we need to be on the same page when we tell them what happened."

"You're right," Evelyn said. "And I think it would be wise for us to tell the cops that when you came into the room, Cedric was on top of me, choking me. He got distracted when he saw you, and that's when I was able to reach for the statue and hit him across the head. He fell to the side, and I rushed into the bedroom to get the gun. He continued to charge at me, so I shot him. That's not completely the truth, but it's close enough to it."

I moved my head from side to side, refusing to put all the blame on Evelyn. "We've got to come up with something else. You know darn well that I'm not going to let you take the fall for this. Can't we just say that we came into the house together, we thought he was an intruder, and I hit him across the head? Then you went to get the gun, and without knowing who he was, you shot him?"

"That makes no sense," Kayla noted. "The police would never believe that, but they may believe that I did it. I took pictures of what Cedric did to me. I could say that I came here to confront him about being with Evelyn and we got into a fight. I could put my fingerprints on the gun and say that I shot my ex-husband, who had been threatening me and had become very abusive toward me after our divorce."

"No, no, no!" Evelyn shouted. "Stop this, okay? My story makes the most sense, and it's closest to the truth. I know the police will probably arrest me, but I'm sure they'll set a bond and I'll be released. I can get a lawyer who can defend me and help me explain why I did what I did. This may not be as difficult as it seems, as long as we all agree to stick to the exact same story. Now, are y'all with me on this or not?"

I looked at Kayla, who seemed to be still on the fence, like me. We didn't have many choices, so for now I decided to go with the flow.

"I don't like it, but I'm with it," I said.

Evelyn turned to Kayla. "What about you, Kayla? Are you with me on this or not?"

Kayla remained silent for at least a minute. She then walked up to Evelyn and gave her a hug. "I don't know what the outcome will be, but I do know that we allowed Cedric to cause a lot of damage in our lives. I hope and pray that this is the right thing to do, and that we will be able to finally move on from this. So, yes, I'm with it too."

Evelyn nodded and swallowed hard as she backed away from Kayla. She took a deep breath before removing her cell phone from her purse and dialing. Within seconds, she went into panic mode and yelled into the phone.

"Hello! Can you please send an ambulance to my apartment! I—I just shot a man who tried to kill me! Hurry, please!"

Evelyn provided the 911 operator with her address, then ended the call. We looked at each other with fear in our eyes. Kayla turned her head to glance at Cedric, and then she started to ramble on and on about his threats and her attempt to go kill him one day. Like me, she was still plotting other options in her head before the police got there.

"I thought that the two of you were on board with me," Evelyn said, with a look of frustration on her face. "We're running out of time. What must I say or do to convince y'all that this is the only real choice that we have? Dumping his body won't work, lying about a fight between Kayla and Cedric won't work, and admitting that Trina struck him on the head will make it look like she and I were out to get him. I know the two of you still have trust issues with me, but this is one time when I'm asking for both of you to follow my lead. Please listen and promise me that we're in this together."

Kayla and I had to make Evelyn that promise. I reached out for their hands, and as we stood in a close circle, we began to pray for guidance. Sirens could be heard in the background, and when we opened our eyes, we looked at each other again.

"Showtime, ladies," Evelyn said. "Let's do this."

Minutes later, numerous police officers swarmed the place. To say that all three of us were nervous as hell would be an understatement.

18

Kayla

As Cedric's body was taken away in a body bag, I was numb. I had flashbacks of when I first met him; of when we were at the hospital, waiting for Jacoby to be born; of when we purchased our new home; and of just the other day, when he beat the crap out of me. So much was going through me now that I couldn't even explain it. I just couldn't explain it. It was as if I was having an out-of-body experience. This all felt like a dream, and in a matter of minutes, I would wake up, feeling a little better. But that didn't happen. This was my reality. Cedric was dead, and they had just put his dead body in the back of a van.

Just like the last time when Paula tried to kill Cedric, people were standing outside, trying to figure out what had happened. Crime-scene tape surrounded the area. Many police officers were walking around, asking questions, and it just so happened that the same evil officer who had been there when Paula Daniels attempted to kill Cedric was there again. But just like the last time, I wasn't guilty. This time, Evelyn and Trina were, but I was hopeful that our story would hold up.

I totally understood how Evelyn felt, and neither of us wanted Trina to get arrested. She had done too much for us. And to be honest, after all that had happened, I didn't want either one of them to go down. Before the police had arrived, I'd told Evelyn and Trina about my plan to shoot Cedric that day. They'd been in awe by what had stopped me, and once again, we had agreed that Evelyn's story was the most believable.

A moment ago she had finished telling two officers how everything had supposedly gone down. Now the officers addressed me and Trina. Trina vouched for her, and so did I. I even lied, saying that I had entered the apartment and had witnessed Cedric charging toward her.

"So you didn't see Mr. Thompson attack her in any way?" one of the officers questioned, with a notepad in his hand, as he looked at me.

"What I saw was my ex-husband rushing toward her with his fist in the air. I didn't see the initial confrontation, but I can assure you that he was in a rage. She had to do whatever she could to stop him," I said.

The two officers looked at each other, then back at us. We all displayed much attitude, because, as we had expected, they were giving us a difficult time.

"Where were the three of you coming from again?" the other officer asked.

Trina quickly spoke up. "Evelyn and I had dinner earlier. We asked Kayla to meet us here. She arrived shortly after we did."

"And the only reason you didn't enter the home at the same time as your friend was that you dumped trash in the Dumpster, correct?" asked the first officer.

Trina nodded. "Right. After putting the trash bag in the Dumpster, I came inside and saw Mr. Thompson choking my friend. I yelled for him to get off of her, and that's when he turned around and saw me standing in the doorway."

"Sure. What was in the trash that you took to the Dumpster?" asked the second officer.

Displaying a frown, Evelyn crossed her arms and quickly spoke up. "Does that really matter? I put one small trash bag in the trunk before we left earlier. I forgot to put it in the Dumpster. If you would like to go to the Dumpster and sift through my tampons, dinner from yesterday, and Diet Pepsi cans, feel free."

The officers were being real jerks. One of them made Evelyn take him to the Dumpster to show him the bag Trina had dumped. Trina and I continued to get hit with several more questions, but, finally, within the hour, the officers wrapped up the questioning.

With sadness in our eyes, we watched a police officer cuff Evelyn's hands behind her back. Trina was standing closer to Evelyn than I was, and filled with emotions, she reached out to Evelyn, grabbing her tightly around the neck.

"I'll be okay," Evelyn said, unable to hug Trina back. "Stop all of this, 'cause I assure you that everything will be fine."

Evelyn had her game face on, but I wasn't so sure that she would be okay. One thing that I did know was that if it weren't for what she and Trina had done, Jacoby could be on his way to jail. Cedric had made that quite clear, and I had certainly taken his word for it.

With that on my mind, I walked up to Evelyn and reached out for her too. Trina had backed away, and I was surprised that the officers didn't separate us from each other. While hugging Evelyn, I leaned in and whispered close to her ear. "We're going to do everything in our power to see that you get released. So no worries and hang in there."

Evelyn displayed a forced smile and nodded. The cops finally pulled us apart and then put her in the backseat of a police car. As it slowly drove off, we watched with heavy hearts as the sight of our BFF faded away.

***

The next several days were some of the most difficult days of my life. I was left to take care of Cedric's funeral arrangements, and I learned that Joy had cleaned out the majority of his bank accounts and was nowhere to be found.

Evelyn's bond had been set at two million dollars. I had a lot of my money tied up in investments, so I really didn't have access to that kind of money right now. The money Evelyn had in the bank, she couldn't even get to. Her assets had been frozen, and we all were very puzzled about that. We couldn't even question anyone about her funds, and since she didn't have a POA listed on her accounts, we were shit out of luck.

The same thing applied to Cedric's house. I wanted to go in there, clean it out, and sell everything. But I couldn't get my hands on anything, unless I trespassed and broke in. I still hadn't decided if I was going to do that yet, but it was an option. Thankfully, he had already paid for his burial; he had requested to be cremated. All I had to do was make sure everything was finalized. Not only that, I had to tell Jacoby that this time, Cedric was truly gone.

Like me, Jacoby had mixed feelings about Cedric's death. There had been good times, as well as bad times. We loved the old Cedric, the Cedric in the beginning. But somewhere down the road, he had got lost. So had I.

"I don't know what to say, Mama," Jacoby said while standing outside, by his car. He scratched his head, then looked down at the ground. "This whole thing is just horrible. How did we get here, and what is going to happen to Evelyn? Are you worried about her?"

"Yes, I'm very worried. But Trina and I are going to do everything that we can to help clear her name."

"Are you sure you want to do that? I mean, she was still fu . . . screwing around with Cedric, wasn't she? I can't believe that after everything he did, she was still messing around with him. Not to mention that you had forgiven her too. The two of you were friends again, weren't you?"

"Yes, we were. It's a long story, and I'll explain it to you later. But her messing around with him or not, Cedric turned into a madman. I think that what Paula Daniels did to him hurt him even more. He wanted revenge, and he didn't quite know where to go to get it. So he took what happened to him out on everybody, even Justin, who just happened to be at the wrong place at the wrong time. Cedric also jumped on me. When I told you I had fallen that day, I'm sure you know I lied."

Jacoby shook his head. "I figured you did. And don't be mad at me for saying this, but this may be a good thing, after all. Eventually, I think we all would have paid the price, and he wouldn't be the only person dead."

"I'm not mad at you at all. I feel the same way. Somebody had to stop him."

Jacoby sighed, then looked directly into my eyes. "Yeah, they did. I guess we should be thankful for Evelyn, huh?"

I agreed. Jacoby came inside and stayed the evening with me. I cooked dinner for us, and then we watched a movie. It felt good spending this time with my son. When I asked how things were going at Adrianne's house, he had nothing nice to say.

"All I can tell you is, I'll be moving back here real soon, if you don't mind. Only for a little while, because it's almost time for me to be on my own. As for Adrianne's mother and her boyfriend, they argue just as much as you and Cedric did. But they argue over the phone a lot. She be accusing him of this and that. Mad at him because he won't come over. Crying because he said this or didn't say that. I mean, does every household have to be like that?"

"No, it doesn't. And every household *isn't* like that. Some people love and respect each other enough, and they have very little problems living together. It's all about finding the right person to be with, and it looks to me that you have found that person in Adrianne. Have you?"

Jacoby smiled. "I think I have. And if we're still together after college and all that stuff, I really want her to be my wife. She's been there for me a lot. I can honestly say that the only two people that I love with all my heart are her and you."

That was a beautiful thing for Jacoby to say. I gave him a squeezing hug and told him that I loved him too.

Two days later I sat in the small sanctuary, paying my final respects to Cedric. Jacoby sat next to me, and even though I shed some tears, he did not shed one. He held my hand the whole time, and when it was over, we shook hands with the fifty people who had shown up and thanked them for coming.

"I'm so sorry for your loss," one of Cedric's business partners said to me. "Be well."

He kissed my cheek, and then another man stepped forward to pay his respects. I didn't know who half these people were, but they all claimed to be some of Cedric's business partners.

"He was a good man," the second business partner said. "A very good man. I can't believe this happened to him."

All I did was nod. A good man, Cedric was not, but I just kept it moving to the next person.

"We lost a gem," his new secretary said. "Cedric was so funny, and our office will never be the same."

Gem? Funny? Now, she had taken it too far. I stood there and heard it all. What I knew was that Cedric had given these people much more respect than he had given me. They didn't even know the man that I knew, but out of respect for him, I stood there without saying a word. Even when one of his tricks walked up and tried her best to hurt my feelings. I didn't know who she was, until Jacoby whispered in my ear that he had seen her with Cedric.

"I'm going to miss Cedric," she said, barely touching the tips of my fingers to give me what she considered a handshake. "We really had a lot of fun together. He sure knew how to keep a smile on my face, and I don't know who I'm going to find to take his place. He's definitely irreplaceable."

"Your search shouldn't be that hard," Jacoby said to her. "Thanks for coming, and good-bye."

All I did was smile. Smiled at her and at everyone else who continued on with their loving stories about Cedric. I seriously wanted to throw up, but this was his moment, so I let him have it.

After it was all over, I picked up the urn and Jacoby grabbed all the photos we had on display. We put everything in the car, then hopped in. I drove, and right at the Missouri River was where I stopped. We got out of the car, and I watched as Jacoby pitched the urn into the dirty, murky water. We gave each other a hug, then watched as the urn drifted away.

May my dear ex-husband now rest in peace, I thought.

19

Evelyn

I could no longer keep my game face on. And after being in this place for almost a week, I was about to go crazy. My bond had been set at two million dollars, cash only, and I had been coming up short. I didn't know how or why all my assets were frozen. It just didn't make sense, and I needed that money like I had never needed it before. I talked to my attorney and Trina almost every day. She was the one who was trying her best to get me out of here. As for my attorney, it seemed as if all his job was, was to figure out how much money he could get from me. Thankfully, however, he had taken my case—in hopes that whenever I got out of here, I would be able to pay him every dime he requested. I hoped so too, but first, I had to come up with the money to post my bail.

There was no question that I had a long way to go with the trial and everything. But if there was a way for me to break out of here today, I would. This jail cell was no way for anyone to live. The so-called beds were hard as hell, the toilets were nasty as ever, the walls and floors were filthy, and don't even let me comment on the smell. There were two other chicks in the cell with me. One of them appeared to be just as scared as I was, and the other thought she was a badass. She had been here and done this before, but like me and the other chick, she was waiting to post bail or get a court date.

"So, you're a murderer," she said while sucking her stained teeth and looking at me as I sat, disgusted, on the bed. "Killed your man because he was dicking down another trick, huh? I don't know why you dumb broads keep finding yourselves in situations like this. Do you know how many women are incarcerated for doing what you did? No dick is worth all that trouble, is it?"

The heavy white chick with long red hair and freckles on her face didn't know what in the hell she was talking about. I started off by not saying a word, but she didn't know anything about me, and so I had to set the record straight.

"It didn't happen like that," I said, rolling my eyes. "I don't kill men over dick problems, but maybe you do."

She got up and stood in front of me, trying to intimidate me. "I don't kill slime-bucket-ass men, either, but I do kill bitches with smart freaking mouths. Would you like to see how I do it?" She slashed across her throat with her finger, then laughed.

Trying to let her know that she couldn't intimidate me, I stood up to confront her. With much force, she pushed me back down.

"Get up again," she said, still sucking those rotten teeth, "and you will never see daylight again, pretty girl."

Just then, a guard walked by and saw her standing in front of me. She tapped the bars with a billy club and gave the fat bitch a warning. "If I come back again and you're still causing trouble, Niecy, I'm going to take you out of there and put you in a place where you belong."

Niecy backed away from me with her hands in the air. "Pretty girl is the one in here harassing me. I ain't said nothing to her, and she's the one who keeps looking at me like she's crazy or something."

"Pretty girl," the guard said to me, "leave Niecy alone. All she wants is some attention, but don't give it to her."

I took the guard's advice by turning myself around to face the wall. Niecy continued to chastise me and the other young lady, as well. I ignored her by closing my eyes and doing only what a place like this would allow me to do—think. I thought about everything, from my ongoing betrayals to Charles. I didn't even know if I would ever get a chance to spend time with my BFF's again, and that was real scary. I couldn't even imagine my life without them. And what about Trina's baby? Would I even be there to see it come into this world, like I was when Kayla had Jacoby? We had all been so tight then. Nothing had been able to keep us apart. I had been so happy for Kayla then, as I was right now for Trina. Just didn't know if I would miss out on everything. I couldn't help but think that there was a chance that I would be in a place like this for the rest of my life. It sure was no picnic, and I was positive that there were more jealous women in prison like Niecy, waiting to start some shit.

My thoughts then turned to Charles and how he had just vanished. I was still puzzled about that situation, but Trina had said she didn't know what was up, because she hadn't been in touch with Keith. I had even asked if she would borrow some money from him. She'd said that she would reach out to anyone that she could, and to my surprise, so had Kayla. Her intentions were to put up some money, but I didn't think she had enough to cover my whole bail. It was a lot for anyone to come up with, and I was so thankful to my BFF's for doing whatever they could do.

I lay sideways on the bed, still facing the wall. It was hot as hell in the cell, and my forehead was dotted with numerous beads of sweat. I curled into a ball, my eyes started to flutter, and I fell asleep.

That night I dreamed that I was free. Dreamed that I was back at home, and Charles was there with me. We were having sex, while Cedric stood at the door, watching us, drinking alcohol from a bottle. He laughed at the thought of me not being able to handle Charles, and Charles laughed too. But as I got up to go curse Cedric, he lifted the bottle he was drinking from and poured the alcohol all over my face. My eyes burned, and when I attempted to open them and escape from my dream, my face was being sprayed with water. That was what I thought it was, until I opened my eyes and saw a bushy-ass, nasty pussy staring at me.

"Oops," Niecy said, laughing. "It's dark in here. I thought you were the toilet."

I totally lost it. I threw that fat bitch off of me and then jumped on top of her. Gripping her hair with my hand, I pounded her damn face, turning it fire red.

"Bitch, do not fuck with me!" I yelled. "Do you hear me? Stop fucking with me!"

Our other cell mate tried to get me off of Niecy, but by that time, several guards had come into the cell to pull me away from her. I kicked and screamed as they dragged me down the hall and then threw me into a tiny-ass room that had filth running down the walls and another shit-stained toilet in the corner.

"Pretty girl, you haven't been here that long to be causing so much trouble," one of the guards said. "It looks as if this may be your permanent home for a while, so you'd better learn how to clamp your mouth shut and cope. 'Cause if you don't, I'll tell you what. You are going to have a difficult time, more than what you will ever expect."

The guard slammed the door, leaving me there with my thoughts. I sat with my back against the wall and my knees pressed against my chest. All I could think about was how fucked up this was. My father might have been proud of this, but surely not my mother—may she continue to rest in peace. I leaned to the side, and with my face on the concrete floor, I had flashbacks of my friendships with my BFF's and thought about all I had done to them. First, I reflected on one of the worst things I had done to Kayla. At the time, I hadn't even recognized how wrong I was.

We were all at Cedric and Kayla's house, and we had just finished dinner. The fellas were downstairs in the basement, playing pool, and me and my BFF's were watching TV there. As soon as Cedric went upstairs, I pretended that I needed to go outside and have a smoke. But realistically, that wasn't the case. I made my way upstairs to find Cedric. The moment I reached the top stair, I saw him standing by the kitchen counter, waiting. He placed one finger over his lips in a gesture for me to be quiet. He then nudged his head toward the garage door and walked toward it. I followed.

Inside the five-car garage was a fleet of lavish cars that belonged to him and Kayla. The only spot that was empty was the spot where Jacoby parked his car. Cedric unlocked his Rolls-Royce and opened the back door. I saw that there was plenty of room in the backseat.

"Are you serious?" I whispered, then giggled. "We're just going to talk, aren't we?"

"Aye, that's all I want to do, unless you have something else in mind, like hooking me up."

We laughed, and I got in the backseat with him. Talking wasn't in our plans. His hands eased up my skirt, and the moment his fingers slipped into my wetness, I turned around and got on my hands and knees. Cedric unzipped his pants and flipped up the back of my skirt. He moved my thong to the side, then filled my hot pocket with his hard, thick meat, which always guaranteed me an orgasm.

"You know I'm jealous," Cedric whispered in my ear while long stroking me from behind. My ass was hiked up, and the sounds of my pussy juices made him aware that he was hitting the right spot.

"Jealous of who or what?" I moaned. "You have no reason to be jealous. I'm the one who is jealous. Jealous of Kayla for getting a piece of this whenever she wants to."

"You can have a piece whenever you want to, too. Just ask for it. And the next time you come over here, leave the broke-looking joker at home. He's an embarrassment, and I know you can do much better."

"I can. That's why I'm doing it with you and not with him."

Cedric tore into my insides and rushed me to the finish line so we could hurry back inside. The car rocked fast from the speed of our action, but as soon as I opened my mouth to react to him busting my cherry, the garage door lifted. Cedric covered my mouth with his hand, and we dropped down low on the floor in the backseat. My pussy was dripping wet from a mixture of our juices, and the feel of Cedric's dick still in me was spectacular.

For whatever reason, I was hoping that Kayla would see us. It wasn't that I hated her or anything like that. I had just lost a lot of respect for an ungrateful bitch who didn't realize or appreciate what she had. Cedric peeked through the tinted windows and whispered to me that it was Jacoby, not Kayla. He waited until Jacoby was inside before he hit me with a few more strokes that tickled my insides and gave me something more to smile about. He had definitely gotten what he wanted, but now it was time for me to get what I wanted.

"Before we go back inside, I need to ask you for a favor. I know you're getting tired of me, but until I find another job, I don't—"

"How much?" Cedric said, then planted a kiss on my cheek.

"Several hundred dollars. Whatever you can spare is fine with me. Anything will help me right about now."

"I'll transfer the money into your account in the morning. And don't be ashamed to ask me for money. We have to look out for each other."

No doubt we did. I was very appreciative of Cedric's generosity. Like always, he came through for me. I intended to always come through for him.

Ten minutes later, Cedric and I entered the house as if nothing had gone on between us. I had the audacity to look my friend in the face, as if I hadn't just fucked her husband and asked him for money.

No words could express how I felt right now, and then I started to think about a time when I had betrayed Trina too.

I thought Keith was alone that day, because Trina had told me she was going out of town. I arrived at his house; the door was unlocked. I didn't even need the key I'd gotten from Bryson's office. The downstairs was pretty dark. Upstairs was too, but I could see light from a television coming from his bedroom. I sauntered up the stairs and could hear soothing jazz music. Apparently, he was trying to set the mood, so I made my way to his doorway. I peeked inside the room and saw him sitting up in bed, with a sheet covering him from the waist down. I knocked on the door and then walked inside. Keith picked up a watch from his nightstand. He was expecting me.

"You're almost ten minutes late. I didn't think you were coming. I was about to fall asleep, because these shows on the television are boring."

"Then Evelyn to the rescue, right?"

I didn't want to waste any time with this. Keith appeared to be on board, and that was a good thing. His eyes locked on me as I removed the belt from my coat. When I peeled the coat away from my shoulders, I saw him suck in a deep breath. I stood before him with no clothes on and ready to handle my business. Keith patted the spot next to him, then cocked his head back.

"Come here," he said softly. "My brother said you were sexy as hell. I guess, now I believe him."

I crawled on the bed like a courageous tiger. Moved so I was face-to-face with him, then leaned in for a kiss. This time, he didn't back away. He didn't reject me, and his mouth opened wide. I couldn't believe what a great kisser he was. No wonder Trina was hooked.

"Sweet lips," he said, holding the sides of my face. He lightly bit my lips a few times and then backed away when the phone rang.

"Sweet pussy too," I replied. "Wait until you taste it."

The ringing phone interrupted us again.

"You may want to go answer that," I said. "Just in case it's you-know-who. The last thing you may want is her showing up here tonight."

Keith shrugged, but he took my advice. He snatched the sheet away from him. Lord have mercy on that body of his.

"I'll go get my phone, and why don't you run to the kitchen to get us some wine out of the fridge?"

I really didn't want any wine, but since Keith was cooperating, what the hell? I went into the kitchen to get the wine and two glasses and then stopped by the bathroom to pee. I could hear Keith going off on somebody over the phone, but then his voice went silent.

It was probably Trina. Then again, she was on a plane to LA. Keith's ex-girlfriend came to mind, so I hurried out of the bathroom to eavesdrop on the conversation.

I returned to the bedroom with the wine bottle and the two glasses in my hand. Keith was back in bed, lying on his side, with the sheet covering him. The television had been turned off, and his cell phone was on the nightstand, ringing again. This time, he ignored it and didn't say a word. I set the wine and the glasses down, then crawled on the bed next to him again. When I pulled the sheet away from him, that was when I got the shock of my life. I eased away from the gun that was aimed right at the center of my forehead, which was starting to build up a sheen of sweat. The look in Trina's eyes was deadly.

"Bitch," she said through gritted teeth, "you got five motherfucking seconds to get your coat back on and get the hell out of my man's house! And if you ever, I mean ever, come back here again, I swear to God that I will blow your damn brains out!"

Trina didn't look like she was bullshitting, so I didn't bother to respond. I kept my eyes on the gun, which trembled in her hand, and carefully eased back off the bed. I bent down to pick up my coat but didn't bother to put it back on. I waved at her and then jetted down the stairs so fast that I almost fell and broke my neck. Keith was waiting for me at the door. His face looked like stone as he held the door wide open. I was too embarrassed to say one word. After I ran outside, he slammed the door so hard that it shook the house. Apparently, he wasn't down with my plans, after all.

Tears welled up in my eyes as I thought about that day. I didn't deserve to have any friends at all, and I was so grateful for Kayla and Trina for sticking by me. Lord knows, they didn't have to. I couldn't even be mad if they decided to scrap all their plans and leave me in here. I deserved this. I had to take the fall for everything, and it was my responsibility to try to make this right. I just didn't know if it was too late for me. Maybe it was.

20

Trina

I was running out of options for Evelyn, but I didn't want to tell her that. Money, money, and more money was what we needed. But since Evelyn had gotten herself into a fight with someone behind bars, I wasn't even able to speak to her. For days Kayla and I pondered what to do next. She had been contributing most of the money, and she was to the point where she couldn't afford to give much more. The only other person whom I could turn to was Keith. Yes, he needed to know about our child, but he wouldn't learn about my pregnancy today. After what Evelyn had done for me, I had to put that situation on the back burner and figure out what I could do to save her. I also didn't want Keith coming back to me because I was pregnant. I wanted him to forgive me totally because in his heart, that was what he wanted too. Since I hadn't heard one word from him, it was obvious that he wasn't there yet.

Keith had money, but it was nowhere near what Evelyn needed. Every little bit helped, so I went to his house to see him. I rang the doorbell, then waited with bated breath for him to come to the door. Looking in through the window, I could see him coming down the stairs. His eyes shifted to his bedroom, then back to me. Before he opened the front door, he looked upstairs again. He then unlocked the door and opened it an inch, wearing nothing but a pair of jeans. A black do-rag was tied around his head, and his colorful tats were in full effect.

"Yes?" he said through the cracked door.

"I need a favor."

He opened the door wider, then stepped outside on the porch with me. It was chilly, but the cold didn't seem to bother him.

"What kind of favor?"

"Before I tell you what it is, I need to elaborate on some of the things you've probably heard on the news about Cedric's murder, and to tell you about my involvement. Do you have time to listen?"

He answered with a nod, and I began to tell him about everything that had happened since I left here. He kept shaking his head and turning it away from me, as if he was disgusted.

"How did you manage to get yourself caught up in that mess?" he said when I finished telling my story.

I started to tell him that I wouldn't even be in this mess had he not put me out of his house. However, I quashed that line of reasoning and went another route instead.

"It just happened, and we both had to defend ourselves. I feel horrible that Evelyn is in there, and the truth is, I should really be in there too. Can you help me with some money to pay her bail? Her attorney is going to want a lot of money, and neither of us has it."

"Evelyn has it. She has it all. Didn't she tell you?"

"I know your mother and father gave her some money for what happened with Bryson, but her accounts are frozen. We can't get access to any of her money, and the banks won't even talk to Kayla or me about those funds. Our hands are tied, and I'm to the point where I don't know what else to do."

Keith was silent; then he released a deep sigh. "Go talk to my father. He should be at home. And if you can't work out anything with him, come back here. I may be able to free up some money somewhere, but it won't be anywhere near what you need."

"I know, and whatever you can do will be much appreciated. Thank you."

Just for the hell of it, I reached out to hug Keith. It sure felt good to be this close to him again, even if it was only for a few seconds. He backed away from me.

"Good-bye, Trina."

My heavy heart just wouldn't let up. I turned around to walk away, but then I pivoted around once again and called his name before he entered the house. This time, I ran up to him and locked my lips on his. I held the back of his head, pulling him to me as I forced him to kiss me. To my surprise, he didn't reject me. But he also didn't allow the kiss to go on for very long. He backed away, but I continued to hold his head and gaze into his eyes.

"I know someone is in there, and I don't care who she is. I don't want to know who she is, but I can assure you that she won't be in your life for long. I'm coming back. You are taking me back, and all I need right now is for you to give me a little hope. All I need is a little hope, and it will surely help after all I've been through."

He stood in silence while looking at me. And when he spoke up, yes, indeed, he gave me hope. "I love you, Trina. I will always love you."

That was enough for me. I left on a serious high. Seemed like I'd waited forever to hear him say those words to me again. I knew he was still trying to cope with what I had done, and it was too soon for me to push. Another woman had him in her possession today, and all I could say was that she'd better enjoy her time with him while it lasted.

***

I rang the loud doorbell, and its chime was like a song being played. It was my hope that Netta wouldn't come to the door, only because I didn't want her looking at me all crazy and questioning me about what had happened between me and Keith. I was sure she knew all about it. But unfortunately for me, I didn't get my wish. She opened the door, displaying a fake smile that I could read through.

"Keith called and said you would be coming over," she said. "Charles's office is upstairs, the second room on the right. But before you go up there, I want to say this to you. When you hurt my sons, you hurt me. And if or when he forgives you, it doesn't mean that I have to."

She walked away. I couldn't even say anything to her, because if any woman had done to my son what I had done to Keith, I would probably be bitter too.

I climbed the curved staircase, which led to numerous rooms on the second floor. Before going into Charles's office, I knocked and he buzzed me in.

"Come in, Trina," he said. "I've been waiting for you."

I entered the office, nervous as hell. Charles sat with his back facing a huge bay window that stretched from one side of the spacious room to the other. Fancy drapes hung from high above, and the old-fashioned desk that he sat behind looked as if it had come straight from the early 1900s. Bookshelves lined the walls, and several computer monitors were all over the place. None of them were on, but CNN played on the TV mounted above the stone fireplace. An American flag on a pole was next to it.

He swung his chair around to face me. Without a doubt, I knew how easily Evelyn had gotten herself caught up. Charles looked just like an older Keith, one without all the muscles and with much more power.

"Have a seat," he said, his eyes scanning me like radar.

I wondered what in the hell he was thinking, but I quickly sat in the chair in front of his desk and started to tell him the purpose of my visit. As I spoke, he kept switching positions in his chair, sighing, and looking at me as if he were looking through me. Not once did his gaze venture away from my eyes. That made me even more nervous.

"That's why I need your help," I said with a cracking voice when I was done recounting my tale of woe. "I'm just as responsible as she is, and I feel obligated to do something and help her out of this."

Charles cleared his throat, and then he sat up straight. He clenched his hands together while resting them on his desk. "You may be at fault for fucking over my son, but you're not at fault for what happened at Evelyn's place. The way I see it, she is one hundred percent to blame for everything, and I haven't made up my mind yet as to how I'm going to deal with her. You see, that woman came into my home with her lover and attempted to extort money from me. I allowed her to think that I wanted that little problem between her and Bryson to go away, but anyone who knows me knows that if I want a problem to disappear, I can make it do so just like that." He snapped his fingers and then got out of his seat.

As he walked over to the bay window to look outside, he slipped his hands into his pockets. "That day, I gave her some money and told her to be gone. I knew that money would eventually wind up destroying her, as that's what happens to people who believe that money can save them. But what she did next really took the cake. She thought she was so good, so special, that she could whip her pussy on me and control me. Yet again, I decided to let her have at it. By design, I messed with her head to put her under my spell. She was definitely hooked, and when I tried to set her free and let her off the hook, she still wouldn't stop there. So now here we are. I have two choices. Would you like to hear what they are?"

I slowly nodded, though deep down I had a feeling that I wasn't going to like where this conversation was going. "Please proceed. And I thank you for sharing this with me."

"You're welcome," he said, then sat in his chair again. He leaned back in it and held up one finger. "I can make everyone believe that your friend is delusional and suffers from a mental illness. It runs in her family, so I won't have a problem convincing anyone that she killed Cedric because he was seeing other women and he didn't want anything to do with her. I will get people to go on that stand and tell a jury that she fantasized about me and our relationship—that it was all made up, that I had never worked where she said I did, and that all of it, every single thing, was part of her wild imagination. And I will say that even though she claimed we had sex, we never did, and she was plotting to kill me too, because I wouldn't get with the program. That, for sure, would send her to a mental institution for the rest of her life."

My stomach hurt so badly, and my throat ached. My heart went out to Evelyn, because this was not looking good. Charles sipped from a glass of water on his desk; then he reached for a pack of gum in his drawer.

"Have some," he said, offering me a piece and then putting one in his mouth.

"No, thank you."

He folded his arms across his chest, then continued. "Option number two goes a little something like this. I can have all her assets unfrozen and allow you to take that money and get her out of this. I would also appreciate it if some of that money got returned to me, but I'm sure—no, positive—that the majority of it will have to be used for her defense. I will put women on the stand who can vouch for her. Who will allow that jury to see what kind of animal Cedric really was and how he deserved to die. Evelyn will look like an abused, distraught, and destroyed woman who had no other choice.

"Even so, I want to be very clear about something. If I decide to go that route, your friend will still have to do some time. I don't want to let her off the hook that easily, and sometimes, people need time to sit and think about all that they've done. When you keep on rescuing them and forgiving them for their mistakes, they tend to take advantage of that. I think that a year in prison . . . maybe two to ten, will do her some good."

I wanted to break down right then and there and just cry. I didn't know how to tell her this, but it was as if there were no other options. I knew she was probably already losing her mind up in there, and I had lost sleep, knowing that she was probably in some kind of hole for getting herself in trouble.

"Mr. Washington, she will not survive in there. I know that she won't, and I'm asking that you please reconsider. She will give every dime of your money back. I will make sure of that, and you will never have to worry about her again. She's had a very difficult life, and many of those things done to her in the past cause her to be this way."

"Believe me when I say I know all about her and her past. And I don't worry about Evelyn at all, nor have I ever lost any sleep thinking about her. Her past is exactly what it is, her past. She used that as an excuse to hurt people, and that kind of shit doesn't fly with me. Being in jail causes people to see things in a different light. I have faith that Evelyn will find that light, and she'll come out of there a reformed person. Stronger, smarter, and humbler than she has ever been before. Nonetheless, I'm delivering my final words to you. They are that there will be no option three. Overnight, I will decide what I believe the best option to be. I'll call you in the morning, or no later than the afternoon. Now, if you don't mind, I have other serious matters to tend to."

In fear of pissing him off and making him change his mind about option two, I remained silent and stood to leave. As I approached the door, he said something to me that made me slowly turn my head.

"Sasha is sweet, isn't she? Good thing you found out she wasn't for you. And just so you know, my son is. Tell him about the baby. He needs to know."

My mouth dropped open, but I didn't bother to elaborate on Sasha or the baby. All I did was reply from my heart, "I know he is for me. That's why I love him with every fiber of my being."

He nodded, then buzzed the door so I could exit.

21

Kayla

Trina came over this morning to tell me about her conversation with Mr. Washington. I was shocked. I hadn't even known about any of this. Yet again, Evelyn had been screwing around with somebody else's husband. I tried not to be so harsh about this, but I knew we all made our own beds and we had to lie in them. I found myself still on the fence about so many things, but there was no question that Evelyn needed my help.

There was a side of me that felt so bad for her. Even one year in prison seemed like a long time. Like Trina, I surely didn't think Evelyn would be able to cope. I was worried about her trying to kill herself and about never seeing her again. I guessed my life wouldn't seem complete without her around, and at this point, at this very point in my life, I started to feel like we were a small yet unique dysfunctional family.

Trina and I waited, on pins and needles, for Mr. Washington's call. I had never met him a day in my life, and I couldn't believe how much authority he had. This was something that you saw on TV or heard about from those who felt that juries were tainted and that people were purposely put on the stand to fabricate stories. If I hadn't heard it from Trina, I wouldn't have believed any of it.

Trina looked at her watch while sitting at the kitchen table. "It's almost one o'clock. Do you think I should try to reach out to him?"

"Do you have his number?"

"No, but I could call Keith to get it."

"Let's wait. If he doesn't call by three, call him."

The next two hours seemed like a whole day. We tried to keep ourselves busy by watching TV and even doing a little exercising. As we sat on some mats, doing yoga, I told Trina how happy I was about the baby.

"I'm happy too. I can't wait, and I don't care if it's a boy or a girl."

"With Jacoby, I didn't care, either. I've always wanted a girl, though, but you know how that story goes."

"I do, but who would have thought that it would end like this?"

"End? Girl, it's just the beginning, especially for you and Keith. You need to tell him that you're pregnant, and whatever your reasons are for not telling him, I'm telling you that they're not good enough. All you're doing is setting yourself up for more chaos between y'all. He's going to be upset about you not telling him, and then y'all will be fighting about that. Keeping secrets has already cost us enough damage, only because one day those secrets all come out."

"I agree, and I will tell him after all this stuff with Evelyn is over. I'm too stressed right now, and believe me when I say that I'm not trying to keep any secrets from him. If I was, Mr. Washington would bust me out. I don't know how he knows so much, but I swear that he knows everything about me, about Evelyn, and probably about you too."

"It sounds like he does, and he's probably thinking that I really need to get a life. In due time I will."

Trina and I started talking about our future plans, but there was no question that Mr. Washington's call was on our minds. And just as we finished exercising, Trina's phone rang.

She snatched it up and hit the speakerphone button so I could hear.

The only thing Mr. Washington said was, "Option two. She'll be released on bail by six o'clock this evening." After that, he ended the call.

"How much time in prison?" Trina yelled. "Damn it! Don't hang up! Tell me how much time!"

Trina had been through so much with her BFF's. If there was any one of us who stood by the other one's side, it was her. She had fought hard to keep our friendships together, and I had rarely told her how grateful I was for her support. In the moment, she seemed very overwhelmed. I reached out to hug her, and she broke down in my arms.

"I want this to be over with," she cried out. "When will all the pain end?"

"Real soon. It will end soon, but we have to stay prayed up and continue to be there for each other. I thank you for always trying to make things right. I know I haven't said it in a long time, but I thank you for everything, Trina. With all my heart, I love you, and you are the best friend any woman could hope for. I know for a fact that Evelyn feels the same way."

"I love you too," Trina said, wiping her eyes.

Sometimes people just needed to hear those three words.

When six o'clock rolled around, we were outside the jailhouse, waiting on Evelyn to come out. Like clockwork, the doors opened, and there she was. A small bag was in her hand. I had never, ever seen her look the way she did. Her eyes looked swollen, her hair was matted, her clothes were slouchy, and her lips looked dry as hell. Not to mention her very pale skin. Trina and I tried to play it down by smiling at her. We hadn't even had a chance to tell her how everything was supposed to go down, and that she would have to spend *some* time in prison. At this point, we still didn't know how much time, but *some* time was set in stone.

We met her halfway, and the first person she hugged was Trina.

"Thank you," she said in a light whisper. "Thank you for everything."

"Thank you too," Trina said. "And you already know why."

Afterward, Evelyn and I hugged too. I hadn't done nearly as much as Trina had done for her, but she knew that I had put up a substantial amount of money for her attorney fees and bail. We were sure that even her attorney would be replaced and that Mr. Washington would assign an attorney who could make things go according to his plan.

"I'm going to get your money back to you," she said to me. "And like always, I owe you."

"Don't worry about it right now. We have other things that we have to deal with. Trina and I will tell you about them in the car."

On the drive back to my place, Trina broke it all down for Evelyn. She remained real quiet. Didn't say much at all. Just listened and listened some more. By the time we reached my place, her only response was, "I guess I just have to do what I have to do."

After that, there was silence.

22

Evelyn

As Trina and Kayla broke it all down for me in the car, I felt numb. All I could say to them that day was, "I guess I just have to do what I have to do," but I didn't feel that way at all. Not after being in that cell with a bully like Niecy. Not after staring at four walls all day, lying in filth, eating garbage, and sitting my ass on those nasty toilets. No, I wasn't ready for that, and I didn't have the guts to tell them how scared I really was. That would worry them. I didn't want to keep stressing them out, and Lord knows, they didn't need any more stress, especially Trina. If something happened to her baby, I would never forgive myself.

So, no question, I needed to take action and do it fast. I was sure there were many more Niecys in prison who couldn't wait to get their hands on me. Therefore, I had to do something . . . anything to get Charles to change his mind. I knew that I was taking a big risk by confronting him, but I didn't have a choice. Trina and Kayla had done so much, and they really couldn't do much more. It was my time to stand up for me, and if Charles had that much control over the outcome, I couldn't sit around doing nothing.

I allowed things to settle down a bit, and a week after I was released from jail, I headed out to find Charles. I had to be careful about going anywhere near his house, but since he was no longer at the office, I basically didn't have a choice. I wanted to catch him when he was by himself. When Netta wasn't around, or Keith or Bryson. It was a Sunday afternoon when I saw the garage door go up and his white Mercedes back out. Thankfully, he was alone. I followed his car, but in no way was I too close. He was too observant, and I knew he would see me, even with my dark shades on and a scarf tied around my head. I had a nice little dress on, as if I had just come from church. My face was makeup free, but I did have on loud red lipstick, which gave me a different look altogether. I glanced in the rearview mirror to make sure no one was following me, and then I looked straight ahead, where I could see Charles making a left to get on the highway.

He drove for about twenty minutes or so and then got off at the Delmar exit, heading toward the Loop. Minutes later, he parked his car and then went inside an Italian restaurant. I waited for a few minutes, just to see if he would be dining with someone. But as I looked through the window, I saw him sitting alone. He glanced at his watch, and when I saw him look toward the door, I figured I'd better hurry up, because maybe he was waiting on someone. I went inside, and as Charles's head was lowered—he was looking at the menu—I slipped into the booth. He slowly lifted his head, and as usual, the pearly whites didn't show.

"I figured you were coming," he said. "I just didn't know when. What do you want, Evelyn? And please make it quick, because I am expecting someone."

I was a little nervous, but I came to say what I had to. "I don't know how quick I can make this, but I really need your help. Trina told me how all of this is supposed to play out, but I can't do this. I can't spend any more time in that place, and if we can work out some kind of deal where I don't have to go back there, I—I will do anything."

"I'm sorry to hear about what you can't do, but there's really not much else that you can do for me. And the last time we tried to work out a deal, it was in your favor, not mine. I don't like to keep negotiating with people who continue to make me feel like a loser. At some point, I have to come out a winner."

"But this isn't about winning or losing. This is about my life." I couldn't help that I started to get emotional. "My life, Charles, and I want it back. I've changed. This entire experience has changed me. I totally get it now. Going to prison will do me no good. It will destroy me and make me bitter. Right now, I'm good. I'm so good, and all I want to do is go live my life in peace."

Charles removed several napkins from the napkin holder, then gave them to me. There was a soft spot in him, for sure. I was trying my best to reach it.

"It's too late for tears, Evelyn. You've been given too many opportunities to correct yourself, and you haven't. I said the same thing to Bryson, and when shit starts to affect me, and I have to inject myself into these little petty matters that I don't have time for, well, it upsets me. I get angry, and, unfortunately, some people have to pay."

I wondered what had happened to Bryson after our meeting that day, because I hadn't seen him. I really didn't have time to inquire about him, but I still asked.

"How did Bryson pay? Where is he? And please know that I have already corrected myself. You just don't know how different I am. I'm loving the new me, and you would be proud of how much I've changed. My friends are proud of me too, and I know you've spoken to Trina about me. She told you everything, didn't she? She believes in me, and I need for you to believe in me too."

Charles snickered, then rubbed the long hair on his chin. He stared at me. I stared at him. Seconds later, he got up and stood next to me. Immediately, my eyes shifted to his package, then to his lips, which found their way to mine. As his tongue entered my mouth, I made mine dance with his. The kiss was intense, and with my eyes closed, I savored every minute of it. I hoped that he did, as well.

"What was that for?" I said softly when he backed away from me. He sat back down, then released a deep sigh.

"As expected, you failed the test, and my point should be much easier to grasp now. The new you won't be discovered until you hit rock bottom. You're not there yet. I assure you that you're not there. You're just trying to say and do all the right things to get me to change my mind. Allowing me to have my way with you is not the route to go. Throwing your pussy at me won't work, Evelyn, and you need to stop believing that it can get you whatever you want."

"I did not just attempt to throw anything at you. You're the one who kissed me. I went with the flow because I'm always happy to see you and I do have some feelings for you. What's the big deal here?"

"I'm sorry if you're too blind to see what it is, and I don't have much time to help you figure it out. The bottom line is, no matter what you say or do, my decision stands. I will not change my mind, but I do have a few suggestions for you. Don't spend the next several months of freedom worrying about where Bryson is. Like you, he was given an opportunity to correct himself, and he didn't. He's somewhere thinking real hard about his mistakes, and I'm going to give you a chance to do the same.

"Until then, make a bucket list and tackle some of the things you have always wanted to do. Spend time with your friends and enjoy your freedom, while you have it. Don't waste another day by following me around, and if you're really a changed woman, get on your knees every day, afternoon and night, and thank God for your friends.

Thank Him that you're still alive after all the dirt that you've done. None of us are perfect, Evelyn, but you still have a lot of soul-searching to do. Good luck, and be sure to choose your battles wisely while you're incarcerated. Doing so will help you stay alive."

Charles exited the booth, then left the restaurant. I sat there, as if cement had been poured over me. In that moment, it finally hit me that this was, indeed, a done deal.

The next several months played out exactly as Charles wanted them to. An attorney was hired to represent me, and he coached me on everything to say, especially when I was put on the witness stand to defend my actions. During the trial several ladies whom I didn't even know and had never seen in my life got on that stand and cried their hearts out about what Cedric had done to them. Charles even went to the extreme of putting Paula Daniels on the stand. She really put on an act. She had the jury in awe when she cried as she told the courtroom about how badly Cedric had beaten her one day.

"My entire body was black and blue," she said. Her lips quivered as she spoke. "He tried to stomp the life out of me, and if it wasn't for my neighbor, I would be six feet under."

Some of the jury members, the ones who hadn't been bought, had tears trapped in their eyes. Paula became so overwhelmed while telling how things had gone down between her and Cedric that a police officer was asked to carry her out of the courtroom.

Kayla was then asked to take the stand. She spoke about how loving Cedric was and then confessed to him beating her too. "I didn't know what was going on," she said. "He turned into a man that I hadn't witnessed the whole time I was married to him. I truly believe that my ex-husband would've killed me that day, because something inside of him snapped. I don't know what it was, but he snapped."

"Did he ever threaten you or put his hands on you after that?" my attorney asked Kayla.

"No, but he called to threaten my son. I was also worried about Cedric hurting my son."

"Thank you, Mrs. Thompson. Thanks for your time."

The arrogant prosecutor approached Kayla with a spiral notebook in his hand. We already knew how all of this was going to play out, and he did his best to make it look good for the jury members who weren't part of the plan and simply for the record.

"Mrs. Thompson, you sit there and act as if you hated your husband. But the fact is, even up until he was murdered by your best friend, you still loved him, didn't you?"

"I loved him as a person, but I wasn't in love with him anymore."

"Really now? I read from a journal that you wrote in prior to his murder, and you say right here that you love him with all your heart. That you wished the two of you had stayed married, and that's why you would never give up your married name."

"That's not true. I decided to keep that name for financial reasons and other reasons that have nothing to do with still being in love with him."

"Maybe that's not true, but it is true that you and your friend shared your husband, isn't it?"

"At one point in the marriage, yes, I did share, without knowing it."

"And that same friend killed your husband, didn't she?"

"Yes."

His voice got stern and louder. "Mrs. Cedric Thompson, did you have anything to do with your husband's murder?

Did you pay your friend to pump three bullets into his chest, bash his head, and kill him!"

Kayla remained as calm as ever, just as she'd been advised. "No. No, I didn't have anything to do with my ex-husband being killed. And in future, please do not address me by his name."

The prosecutor rolled his eyes, then looked at the judge. "No further questions."

My stomach was tight the whole time Kayla spoke. She did good, and I was so relieved. I awaited my time on the stand, and it happened later that day. At first I was nervous, but my attorney helped to put me at ease. He bombarded me with question after question. He asked me to explain how it all went down that day. He also asked me to speak about my ongoing relationship with Cedric. You'd better believe that I made it sound horrific. I saw one of the jury members clench her chest and another shake her head. Even though Charles had crafted this trial, I seriously thought that when all was said and done, the jury would find me not guilty of murder in the second degree. However, less than a week later, they did.

I still did not know my ultimate fate, and I guessed that Charles intended to put me on pins and needles as I stood before the judge, who was responsible for delivering my sentence. He gave his spiel, which went in one ear and out the other. All I wanted to hear was the number of years I would get for murdering Cedric.

"I sentence you to five years in the—"

After hearing the words *five years*, I fainted.

23

Trina

This past year had been interesting. Keith and I were taking things one day at a time, and I was so grateful to him for giving me another chance. He wasn't completely over what I had done to him, but he was thankful, as well as excited, about his newborn son. I hadn't seen Keith this happy in a long time, and it made me regret that I hadn't gotten my act together sooner. I, too, was happy, and our little boy changed our lives in ways that neither of us had thought was possible. Our anniversary was in one month. I was one sista who was hoping and praying that my man would propose to me. I kind of sensed it, and you'd better believe I was keeping my fingers crossed.

As for Kayla, she had stuck with her Alcoholics Anonymous classes and had been sober for months. We were spending a lot of time together while Evelyn was away, and my bond with Kayla was stronger, as well as unbreakable. She and Jacoby had been getting along better too. He was trying to finish up school, and I suspected that he was ready to move out of Kayla's house for good and live on his own. Kayla had said that he hadn't mentioned much else about Cedric, and she had also mentioned that he wanted to have his last name changed. She felt some kind of way about it, but I reminded her that it was time for her to let go and let Jacoby do him.

Evelyn's situation, however, had been turned out to be much more complicated than we had originally thought it would be. We were disappointed about the five-year sentence, especially since the bottom line in the case was that it was an act of self-defense. I'd felt that there was no way that I could sit back and let Evelyn do five years for something I'd had my hands in too, and so as soon as she was to have visitors, I'd spoken to her and Kayla about coming clean and telling the police about my involvement.

"Hell, no," Evelyn said, looking at me tearfully that day as she sat behind the thick glass. She was dressed in an orange jumpsuit, there were bags underneath her eyes, and stress was written all over her frowning face. "This is over with, Trina. It's time for us to move on, and five years will come and go just like that." She snapped her fingers, but I wasn't buying what she was trying to sell me.

"You don't have to put on your game face for me. All I'm saying is—"

She quickly cut me off. "All I'm saying is people are listening, so it's best that we talk about something positive." Her eyes traveled to my stomach. She cracked a tiny smile. "Have you decided what you're going to name the baby yet? I'm good with picking names, and if it's a girl, feel free to name her after me."

Evelyn was trying to change the subject, but I needed her to be on the same page with me when I decided to go to the police and tell them what had really happened.

"I haven't decided on a name yet, but I have decided to go to the police. We—"

"If you do, I'll make you look like a liar. And if you say one more word about this, Trina, this conversation is done."

I ignored Evelyn's threat, and as I continued to make my case for wanting to tell the truth, she glared at me through the window before placing the phone on the hook. She swallowed hard, then moved away from the window. I sat, full of emotions, not knowing what else to do. Kayla was in the car, waiting for me. After her prior conversation with Evelyn, Kayla had advised me to stick with the plan.

"If she doesn't want anyone to know the truth about what really happened that day, then let it go," Kayla had said. "Going through another trial will be difficult for all of us, and the outcome could be even worse than it is now."

That had, indeed, been a possibility, but remaining silent had been difficult to do, especially after I'd started getting letters from Evelyn that were nothing nice to read. She kept talking about wanting to kill herself, and about her ongoing arguments and fights with others. And after being in the hole so much, it appeared that she had begun to realize that she just wasn't going to win in a place like that. There were too many women trying to be the boss, and she had to sit back and give them their crown. I had responded by telling her how much I regretted not telling the police the truth. I'd also mentioned that it was not too late for me to speak up, but after my third letter to her in which I declared my intentions to do something, her letters stopped, and the fourth one I wrote came back marked RETURN TO SENDER. I thought that something bad had happened to her, but it was obvious that she wasn't down with my plan and had decided to ignore me. I had nowhere else to turn but to Keith. He had been against me going to the police, as well, and had kept reminding me of the dire consequences.

"This is one time I will have to agree with Evelyn," he said as we discussed my options one day. "What's done

is done. Evelyn will be okay, but you won't be if you keep stressing yourself like this. You've got to take care of yourself, baby. And what about us? We deserve to be happy, and for once, I want you to think about how important it is for you to be at your best for our child."

I squeezed my aching forehead, trying to soothe a headache that wouldn't go away. "I'm trying to be the best person I can be, but this is hard, Keith. I wish there was something I could do to get her out of there sooner. I don't think nobody understands how painful this has been for all of us. Kayla and I both feel as if we haven't done enough. Yes, Evelyn brought a lot of this on herself, but the truth is, we're like family. They are my family, Keith, and we have been through so much."

Keith could see how wounded I was. He embraced me, then planted a soft kiss on my forehead. "I do understand. Some bonds can never be broken, but I want you to make me a promise. If you promise to start taking care of yourself, and our child, I'll reach out to my father and see if there is anything he can do. I don't know if he can do anything, but we'll see."

I rested my head against Keith's chest, praying for some kind of miracle.

The miracle arrived almost a year and a half later, when Kayla and I were informed that Evelyn would be released. With much enthusiasm, we drove to the prison to get her and parked right outside the gates through which she would soon walk free. I couldn't wait to see my BFF, and as we stood outside my car, waiting for Evelyn, we tried to guess how she would look.

"I bet she done cut off all her hair," Kayla said while holding out her pinkie finger. "How much do you want to bet?"

"No way. Evelyn's hair is probably somewhere down her back. I'm sure her nails are all polished, and she may come out here with a suit on."

"See, I disagree. I think she done gave all that up."

"Girl, this is Evelyn we're talking about. I don't care where she's at. You know she is going to do her best to look good."

We laughed, but as time ticked away, Kayla bit her nails, all the while keeping her eyes on the door through which we expected Evelyn to exit. She was getting just as nervous as I was, especially since another prisoner had made an exit about thirty minutes ago. We were so sure that Evelyn would be coming soon. But after fifteen or so more minutes, we started to get worried. I didn't know who to call in order to find out why this was taking so long, but just as I was reaching for my phone to call Keith, the steel door to the prison came open. I could see Evelyn from a distance, and just as I had predicted, her hair was parted down the middle and she sported a long ponytail that stopped midway down her back. She wore a white T-shirt and a pair of baggy jeans that did nothing for her figure. She also looked as if she had picked up some weight, but it wasn't a lot. A smile was on her face, and as she got closer, she started to laugh while strutting on the pavement.

"I's free!" she shouted as the gates parted. "Y'all hear me, ladies? I's free!"

She started skipping her way to us, and then she stopped to do the cabbage patch. We could see that her sense of humor had improved. That made us feel good, and the smiles on our faces showed it. She held out her arms, then grabbed me and Kayla around our necks when she reached us. She kissed my cheek first, then Kayla's.

"I missed the hell out of y'all," she said tearfully. "I dreamed night after night about this day, and all I wanted to do was wrap my arms around my BFF's again."

Totally relieved, we knew exactly how she felt. Our arms were wrapped tightly around her, as well, and what an amazing day this was for us. I mean, if our friendship could be mended after all that we had endured, surely, other friendships could be too. Not all, but certainly some. . . .

Book Club Questions

1. Is it okay to forgive someone for cheating, or should you just abandon the relationship or friendship?
2. Do you think that Evelyn has changed by the end of the novel?
3. Should Kayla have told Cedric that Jacoby paid Paula Daniels to kill him?
4. Should friends be held to the same standards as someone you date? Why or why not?
5. How do you feel about forgiving people? Were Trina and Kayla right or wrong for forgiving Evelyn?
6. How do you feel about Trina's relationship with Keith? Was he right to forgive her?
7. Could you see yourself involved with a man like Charles Washington, if he wasn't married? Why or why not?
8. Who is your favorite character?
9. Could you ever see yourself taking the fall for a friend? Why or why not?
10. What is one of the worst things a friend has done to you, and how did you overcome it?
11. What message did you get from reading this book?

ORDER FORM
URBAN BOOKS, LLC
97 N. 18th Street
Wyandanch, NY 11798

Name (please print):_________________________________

Address: _________________________________

City/State: _________________________________

Zip: _________________________________

QTY	TITLES	PRICE

Shipping and handling-add $3.50 for 1st book, then $1.75 for each additional book.

Please send a check payable to:

Urban Books, LLC

Please allow 4–6 weeks for delivery